Stink City

Stink City

Richard W. Jennings

Houghton Mifflin Company Boston 2006

Walter Lorraine Books

For Ashle, Maddie, Faith, Halle, and Aidan

Walter Lorraine (wn) Books

Copyright © 2006 by Richard W. Jennings

All rights reserved. For information about permission
to reproduce selections from this book, write to Permissions,
Houghton Mifflin Company, 215 Park Avenue South,
New York, New York 10003.

www.houghtonmifflinbooks.com

Library of Congress Cataloging-in-Publication Data

Jennings, Richard W. (Richard Walker), 1945-
  Stink City / Richard W. Jennings.
     p. cm.
  "Walter Lorraine books."
  Summary: As fifteen-year-old Cade gets involved in animal rights
activism in his struggle to atone for the suffering of fish used in his
family's smelly catfish bait business, his neighbor Leigh Ann tries to
keep him out of trouble.
  ISBN-13: 978-0-618-55248-1
  ISBN-10: 0-618-55248-0
  [1. Catfishes—Fiction.] I. Title.
  PZ7.J4298765St 2006
  [Fic]—dc22

                                                    2006005863

Printed in the United States of America

MP 10 9 8 7 6 5 4 3 2 1

My thanks to Tim Janicke, editor, *Star Magazine, The Kansas City Star,* for sharing this story with his readers throughout 2006; to *The Kansas City Star* and The Writers Place—Midwest Center for the Literary Arts—for assistance provided by the William Rockhill Nelson Award for fiction; and to Miranda Bennett, Sydney Stoll, Alexandria Copani, Alison Connelly, and Geoffrey Jennings for their observations and comment, without which I could not have created the book that you hold in your hands.

— R.W.J.

A Long Time Ago in a Lake Far Away

Sploosh!

The stinkbait plug hit the top of the choppy water and sank slowly to the bottom, sending up a tiny cloud of mud dust as it alighted silently near a rusted-out Kelvinator refrigerator, with its door removed, an artifact that some Ozark hillbilly, believing all bodies of water to be God's trash dumpsters, had cast into the lake many years before.

Inside the icebox, dozing as he did for twenty-two hours out of every day, was Old Foster, the biggest, meanest, ugliest catfish in the forty-eight contiguous states, a gruesome-looking member of a rare sub-species known to a handful of foreign-speaking, American-trained ichthyologists as a horned pout.

Among ordinary sports fishermen, Old Foster had grown to mythic status. Fathers told their sons about him. The sons told *their* sons. (The mothers, meanwhile, attempted to avoid getting involved in the conversation by reading home decorating catalogs and baking simple, heartwarming treats using the dough for Pillsbury crescent rolls.)

Of the many men determined to catch Old Foster and bask in the bright, unnatural, and presumably lucrative light of fame, none was more determined than a man recently retired from government service named Earl Emerson Carlsen.

For four years, forsaking traditional family obligations, Earl Emerson Carlsen had been experimenting with various concoctions to create the perfect catfish bait, something he hoped that even the elusive Old Foster could not resist.

For each day of those four frustrating years, Earl Emerson Carlsen had woken up before sunrise, rubbed a plug in a newly created recipe of foulness, putridity, and breath-sucking stink, and sat quietly in his little aluminum bass boat in the semidarkness to wait for Old Foster to come to breakfast.

And for four seemingly wasted years, Earl Emerson Carlsen had returned home empty-handed.

But Earl Emerson Carlsen was no ordinary fisherman, and, for that matter, no ordinary man.

If he was feeling discouraged, he never let it show. Success in any field, he knew, is based on personal obsession. No matter how many times you fail, you must never, ever give up.

If you want to be the world's greatest baseball player, for example, you must play baseball all the time until you *are* the greatest.

If you hanker to become the world's most admired ballerina, then you must dance, dance, dance, and dance.

If you want to dominate the business of retailing throughout the world, you can never stop lowering prices, or wages, or employee benefits. (Arguably, at some point, you must give your goods away.)

And if you want to catch Old Foster, you must spend every day of your life sitting patiently in your boat.

Such aspiration is not an avocation. It is not a job. It is not even a duty. It is nothing less than a religious calling.

Earl Emerson Carlsen knew this, even if his wife and family and neighbors did not.

A flock of geese flew over the lake well before sunrise, unseen, but their raucous calls were heard by Earl Emerson Carlsen, who, as usual, was rocking in the breeze in his lightweight boat.

Something about the day portended change, not unlike the dramatic arrival of Mary Poppins one morning in London so many years ago, flying in so unexpectedly on a simple but sturdy black umbrella.

But on this particular day, just as the sun peeked over the shimmering cottonwoods, an overwhelmed Old Foster took the compact lump of unusually aromatic bait, and Earl Emerson Carlsen's life changed forever. And although Earl Emerson Carlsen didn't realize it at the time, so did the life of his grandchild, Cade Carlsen, yet unborn.

"Eureka!" cried Earl Emerson Carlsen, as Old Foster pulled him overboard into the chilly waters.

"I have found it!"

The Shadow of Your Smell

You know how every house you enter has its own

distinctive aroma—a family smell—that its occupants seem not to detect?

When you first step inside, some houses greet you with a blend of moldy basements, piled-up laundry, neglected bathrooms, and cats, while others are thick with the synthetic emissions of spring-scented bath soaps and orange cleanser.

Some people's houses smell like barrooms, with cigarette smoke trapped in the draperies and the people themselves cologned with alcoholic beverages. Other houses I've been in smell of well-worn shoes, cooked cauliflower, fresh paint, Christmas, bug spray, and, in one particular case that I will never, ever forget, impending death.

No two households smell the same, and while I'm sure that I will never know the truth about mine, when my father was here, the garage—the only room that was truly his—smelled strongly of cigars. Since then, as a household of two hygienic, fastidious women—me and my mom—we put a lot of faith in vanilla PlugIns.

But this is not about me. This is about my neighbor—the poor kid.

There's nothing wrong with Cade Carlsen's looks. He has blond hair, brown eyes, reasonably clear skin, and in profile his face resembles an ancient Mediterranean statue before its nose got knocked off by barbarians.

Cade is shorter than the other kids at school, but at fifteen, it's possible that he's still growing. Time will tell. And it's not like he's broke or selfish or mean-spirited or anything. Thanks to a thriving family business—the root of his troubles—he has a tidy cache of spending money with which he is quite generous, for all the good it does him socially.

No, the problem with Cade Carlsen isn't his appearance or his financial circumstances or his personality.

It's that he smells bad.

In fact, Cade's house and his whole stinking family smell bad—gawd-awful, in fact—and there's no getting around it.

Anyway, the stink is not the worst part.

The worst part is that thanks to coincidences of birth and geographical proximity, I am Cade Carlsen's best friend. This is not a situation that I would have selected for myself.

Thankfully, a sinus condition due to airborne country allergens permits me to bear this otherwise unbearable burden much of the time.

As with all things, there is a logical explanation for Cade Carlsen's deplorable situation, which I can sum up in two words:

Stink City.

Stink City is the registered trademark of the most effective catfish bait ever devised by the wily mind of man. It is also quite possibly the single most noxious-smelling substance on this planet. Once you get it on you, it's impossible to get it off.

On Saturdays during fishing season, just as soon as he gets off work, Cade takes a shower.

It's hardly worth the bother.

You know how dogs like to roll in stink? You know how their sense of smell is a million times more sensitive than humans'? According to scientists, dogs can detect odors that we humans don't even know exist. No less an expert than the Page-A-Day® calendar reports that dogs can smell the subtle changes in our body chemistry when we go from feeling happy to feeling sad, or from being well to being sick.

That's why I recommend that if your dog should ever run away, before you go posting a reward, wait a few days, then call the Carlsens at 1-555-CATBAIT. (This is a free call.) Within the four-state region, sooner or later, most itinerant canines follow their noses to the powerful aroma emanating from the Carlsens' place.

That's where the Carlsens make their ghastly goo, in back of their house, in the secrecy of a steel shed on a thousand-acre spread of prairie grasses next door to my mother and me.

Lucky us.

But, as Cade points out, they were there first. In fact, it was Cade's great-grandfather who started the company after he retired from his high-ranking government job. Today the old geezer is one hundred and seven years old, which makes him one of the oldest people in the world.

Every year on his birthday, the *Pottersville Post* runs Earl Emerson Carlsen's picture on the front page. On my doorstep, thankfully, it smells like fresh newsprint.

The old man is quite wrinkled, but his creases are only skin-deep. His great-grandson, on the other hand, is fully divided, a boy at odds with himself.

Cade Carlsen has a worried mind that he can never shut off. Among his more earnest anxieties is a concern for the fate of catfish.

And why?

"Fish feel pain," Cade declares.

A Woman's Burden

"Fish feel pain," Cade Carlsen, the Stink City heir apparent, repeated as we sat together in the back of the school bus. "It's a proven scientific fact. It's simply not right to hook them."

"If you say so," I agreed, wiping my runny nose with the back of my hand.

A fish's ability to register pain was a subject I knew something about, having followed the controversy through the pages of the *Pottersville Post* for some time.

For years, few people bothered to take the fish's point of view seriously. A fish's nervous system is too primitive for it to suffer from a fishhook in its lip, the experts agreed. Even dropping a lobster into boiling water isn't torture, they claimed, despite the racket made by doomed crustaceans thrashing around in the pot. Animals such as these just don't have the brains for pain, authorities pointed out.

Uh-huh.

Research scientists in Great Britain disagreed. They discovered a number of receptors in the heads of fish that resemble pain receptors in humans and, in controlled experiments, observed behavior in fish consistent with human reactions to torture, include writhing around uncontrollably and attempting to scream.

In other words, big brains or little brains, if you stick 'em, boil 'em, cut 'em, or leave 'em out to dry on the dock, it's going to hurt like the dickens.

So Cade Carlsen was not necessarily mistaken when he decided to side with the fish. His mistake— or series of mistakes, as it turned out—was in how he went about it.

On impulse, he joined the Foundation for Ichthyology Studies and Humane Treatment of Aquatic Life Everywhere (the initials spell out FISH-TALE), headquartered in Springfield, where shortly after his check cleared he was named Junior Regional Chairman, Freshwater Division, meaning, as I interpret such matters, that he was among the organization's biggest saps.

"If your parents ever find out what you did, you're going to be in a lot of trouble," I warned him. "Their livelihood depends on people fishing with a clear conscience, unless, of course, there's beer involved."

"No adult should have a clear conscience," Cade retorted. "Besides, do you think my parents would prefer I sit on my butt and do nothing?"

"Of course they would," I told him. "That's what fishing is."

I might have been more sympathetic to his gesture if it had involved cottontail rabbits, mallard ducks, white-tailed deer, or even butterflies—anything but catfish.

With their forked tails, squashed faces, wide, pale, bloated lips, squirmy whiskers, and patches of fat, catfish are nasty, slimy, lurking bottom feeders. If it sinks and it stinks, a catfish will eat it, and the deader it is, the better it tastes to a catfish.

In my opinion, the species is little more than a wet, featherless variation on the visually offensive turkey vulture. The catfish's only real attribute is that, when breaded and deep-fried, it tastes good.

I like mine with tartar sauce.

But fate insisted that this foolish boy be my friend, so as we walked from the bus stop down the gravel road on a cold February afternoon with a pack of stray dogs sniffing at his aromatic heels, I tried a different tack.

"Did you ever wonder why fish have such disgusting names?" I asked him.

"What do you mean?" Cade answered. "What's wrong with 'catfish'?"

"Well, that one's not so bad, but what about crappie, shad, scup, roach, goggle eye, and sucker?" I said.

Cade displayed a blank look.

"Okay," I said. "Then try shovelhead, hammerhead, chub, hick, hogchoker, toadfish, lizardfish, hagfish, and snook. Those are hardly names you'd want to give your children."

"I don't plan to have any children," he announced, kicking a rock into the ditch, where it sent a hapless hidden toad scurrying for the safety of the underbrush.

"No children?" I responded. "Not ever?"

"What would be the point, Leigh Ann?" he replied. "It's such a cruel world. They'd only wind up being unhappy."

Hmm, I thought. *This boy is seriously depressed.*

What is it about being born female? Are we destined to become nothing more than guardian angels, school-teachers, diaper changers, and nurses?

Whatever the circumstances, I realized that it was up to me—and me alone—to straighten out this distraught, confused, and very stinky young boy.

All right, I said to fate. *If you insist.*

Trouble in the Wind

Poor, blue Cade Carlsen.

The boy was in a serious funk.

Fortunately, he had me in his life: Pollyanna, Leigh Ann of Sunnybrook Farm, Little Goody Two-Shoes.

I scanned our surroundings for something cheerful to introduce into the conversation. On either side of the road, tiny yellow crocuses clustered like Lilliputian ballet dancers celebrating the first breath of spring.

I knew better.

Crocuses are foolhardy flowers, impatient and overeager, no more reliable as harbingers of an improvement in the climate than that silly what's-his-name, the celebrity groundhog in far-off Pennsylvania.

Phil, that's it.

The fat little fool.

You can't tell me he doesn't feel pain. Heck, that stupid rodent feels the first whiff of chilled air on his wide, wattled back and immediately ducks for cover.

The fact is, winter rages on, regardless of what these daredevil crocuses do.

If you want to know when spring is near, the only sure sign is this: the lake is warm enough for you to catch a catfish.

Dang! I realized. *No wonder that boy is going around with a hangdog face!*

Cade has every reason in the world to feel gloomy. Once the daffodils appear, Cade's family's factory will start cranking out Stink City catfish bait by the caseful, and like so many rural families everywhere, the Carlsens will force their sensitive firstborn and only child to provide cheap, captive, round-the-clock manual labor under the most deplorable conditions you could imagine.

What a world! I thought. *Catfish may be on the bottom, but they're still looking down at kids.*

As to what goes into the nauseating glop that the Carlsens make, well, that's a highly classified secret. Neither Cade nor his parents know the precise formula. That's the crafty great-grandfather Earl Emerson Carlsen's hold over them all.

Knowledge is power.

So are secrecy, ruthlessness, and a disdain for the aspirations of one's closest relations. The old man ran the place with an iron fist and nobody dared to challenge him.

I, on the other hand, being unrelated and thus independent, keep my eyes peeled for clues.

Based on the labels on barrels I've seen stacked around the factory and rusting into razor-sharp detritus down in the creek, some of Stink City's ingredients are cheese mold, rancid hog brains, turkey blood, rat vomit, bat guano, cigar butts, Old Spice, and squid oil, plus some unidentifiable stuff from containers marked only with Chinese characters.

If you leave a twelve-ounce jar of Stink City open for a few hours, the stuff bubbles up and releases a powerful, possibly lethal, gas. Cade calls it Fart-in-a-Jar, but the truth is, it reeks much more than any accidental human exhaust.

To my way of thinking, it's the worst smell on earth.

There are some who say that the stink that comes from the blowhole of a breeching whale is the worst smell on the planet, and I suppose that's possible, but how many people have had firsthand experience?

Anyway, since there's never been a whale within a thousand miles of Pottersville, I'm sticking with Stink City catfish bait as the international standard.

On the days when the factory is in full operation, none of the Carlsens is allowed inside Guastello's

Dollar Cheaper supermarket. Instead, they have to call in their order and wait outside in the parking lot for Mrs. Guastello or one of her daughters to bring their stuff to them.

Even today, I found myself skipping a few paces ahead of Cade, who is a fast walker, trying to stay upwind of my best friend and closest neighbor.

"You do know, Cade," I called back over my shoulder, trying to sound as if the thought had just popped into my head for no particular reason, "that for a scented fabric softener to be effective, you have to add it to the final rinse cycle, don't you?"

"What are you driving at, Leigh Ann?" Cade asked. "What's scented fabric softener got to do with anything?"

Hmm, I thought to myself. *This project is going to take a while.*

Speak of the Devil

In a stale-smelling second-floor one-bedroom apartment in downtown Springfield, Miss Martina Hyde rubbed her gnarled, liver-spotted hands together and cackled at her good fortune.

"Hoop-tee-do," she cried to no one in particular, although the outburst was heard by her pet goldfish, Giorgio, who, to his disappointment, erroneously thought it signaled a forthcoming serving of stinky dried bugs.

Just as it is known that over time married couples come to resemble each other, and dog owners begin to look like their dogs, so it was that, physically, at least, Miss Hyde had much in common with the creatures she purported to protect.

Among these reminiscent features were a squat body, a recessive chin, grayish green spotted skin, and a disarming patch of free-flowing chin whiskers, or lower barbels.

To compensate for her absence of conventional beauty, Miss Hyde dressed flamboyantly, preferring bright, loose-fitting Caribbean-flower muumuus and armloads of clacking plastic bangles. She kept her fingernails painted a glossy fire engine red. Her hair had been bleached so many times that it had neither any discernible color nor any other sign of life. You certainly wouldn't want to get poked in the eye with a strand of it.

Talk about feeling pain!

Hers was a fashion statement that fell somewhere

17

between that of a successful South Florida real estate agent and an aging voodoo priestess in Haiti.

Her vocal reaction to Cade's foolishly generous financial gesture had been delivered in a raspy, mannish voice, the legacy of years of inhaling menthol cigarettes through plastic filters. Sensing an opportunity for a prize catch, she reached for a note card from her special collection.

Dear Mr. Carlsen, she wrote, her handwriting rich, flowery, and falsely suggesting sincerity.

> *Thank you for your kindness. As you know, unless you are a member of the Kansas State Board of Education, life on our planet first emerged from its waters. By your actions, our living ancestors have been granted a day of freedom from dreadful suffering. I enclose a token of my gratitude.*

> *Very truly yours,*
> *Miss Martina Hyde*
> *Executive Director*

Before folding the card, the cover of which reproduced a close-up photograph of a struggling channel catfish impaled through its lip by the gleaming black point of a Gamakatsu Shiner Straight Eye, Miss Hyde inserted a bumper sticker that read FISH FEEL PAIN®.

This was all it took.

Two days later, when Debra Dogwald, the post-mistress, arrived, having just finished a chicken-fried steak at the Pottersville Country Corner Cafe, Cade Carlsen, too, was hooked.

"Leigh Ann," he asked me the next morning, opening his math book to show me the sticker he'd hidden between the pages, "do you think they'll let me put this on the back of the school bus?"

"*Let* you, Cade?" I said. "One doesn't ask school officials for permission. They always say no. If I were you, I'd just do it."

"Well, okay," Cade replied. "If you're sure."

"I'm positive," I told him.

But as big as a bus bumper is, it's never big enough to contain every long-winded, bloviated point of view on every controversial environmental subject. When Cade and I sneaked around to the back of the school bus, we were surprised to see that somebody had beaten us to the prime advertising space. On a series of bumper stickers extending from the fuel tank to the tailpipe was a picture of a laughing catfish twirling a fishhook as if it were a pocket watch on a gold chain, accompanied by this enticing announcement:

SPRINGFIELD CATFISH DERBY
THIRD BIGGEST CATFISH TOURNAMENT
WEST OF THE MISSISSIPPI
MAY 16, 17, 18
MUD LAKE BOAT RAMP
$12,000 IN CASH & PRIZES
FOOD—FUN—FISH—ROYALTY

"I understand everything but the last word," I said. "What do you suppose they mean by 'royalty'?"

"Every year the festival organizers choose a king or a queen of catfish," Cade answered. "In certain circles, it's considered quite an honor. My great-grandfather was the very first to be crowned, Springfield's first-ever King Catfish, but that, of course, was a long, long time ago."

"And there are still people who don't mind being called King or Queen Catfish?" I asked skeptically.

"Apparently," Cade replied. "Traditions die hard."

"Incredible," I remarked as the school bus started up again, blasting ghastly diesel fumes in our faces, an olfactory experience I definitely should add to my growing list of the world's most unpleasant smells.

A Porpoise in Life

The most challenging part of the day at Pottersville High School is lunchtime. This is due to the dubious culinary talents of one man, Chef Ludd, whose last name has never been known, or possibly it is his first name that is not known.

Whichever, Chef Ludd's professional credentials include ten years as head chef for the U.S. Medical Center for Federal Prisoners in Springfield, from which he was lured by a financial contribution from Cade's great-grandfather Earl Emerson Carlsen.

According to the *Pottersville Post,* Mr. Carlsen remarked at the time, "The best lesson that kids of today can learn is to eat the kind of slop I had to eat when I was growing up. It's a real motivator, let me tell you."

Thanks to this misguided intercession, at Pottersville High you will never find hamburgers, pizza, tacos, spaghetti, submarine sandwiches, or waffles on a stick on the luncheon menu. Here, every meal is based on a foundation of watery, sorghum-soaked gruel covered with various flavors of hard-to-identify liquefied matter, providing the student with an ongoing journey through the continents of taste and smell, which, in fact, are one and the same sensation.

With such a selection in the cafeteria, it's easy to understand why many students, Cade and myself included, frequently depend for the midday meal on the colorful vending machines that surround the interior walls of the commons, where virtually every product that is manufactured, canned, boxed, poly-wrapped, vacuum-packed, or bottled by Frito-Lay, Pepsico, the Coca-Cola Company, Keebler, Sara Lee, and Interstate Bakeries, the inventors of Twinkies, was available for a mere pocketful of quarters.

Ironically, today's gruel was flavored with puree of catfish, prepared with a thin corn syrup binder and served with a hard round roll that might have been useful on a bocce ball court, should the school ever decide to install one. (The Guastello family, Potterville's grocery magnates, had once considered underwriting such an endeavor, but they withdrew their offer when the principal insisted that it be named after himself.)

"I can't eat this," Cade whined, setting aside his plate.

"And it's not just because it tastes so bad. Eating catfish goes against all my principles."

"Push it over here," I instructed.

"I mean it, Leigh Ann," he said. "My situation really bothers me."

"Perhaps you're just hungry," I suggested. "Here, take my roll."

"You don't understand," Cade went on. "I just feel so guilty."

"More for me," I muttered between sloppy spoonfuls.

"If only I could figure out a way to make amends," he moaned.

"Good grief, Cade," I said, choking as I attempted to swallow the extra helping of Chef Ludd's latest creation. "Isn't your life challenging enough without taking the heat for your whole misguided family?"

"It's not my life that's important," Cade replied with a plaintive, world-weary sigh. "It's the lower species who can't defend themselves that truly matter."

Not only is he depressed, I thought, *but he's also an idealist. What a terrible combination!*

It's roughly a two-hour drive from Pottersville to Springfield. Sometimes, with highway construction, or bad weather, or a horse-drawn vehicle piloted by one of the area's Amish clip-clopping along the interstate, it's longer, but typically for a trip to Springfield you figure on spending half a day.

That's why I was so concerned when, the following Saturday, after Cade volunteered to go with Stretch Glossup, the Carlsens' handyman, to check on plans for a Stink City exhibit at the upcoming Catfish Derby, they hadn't returned by dinnertime.

"I reckon they got tied up," his father suggested.

"I reckon," I replied.

That night, to pass the time, I watched a special on public TV about the evolution of life in the sea. Starting with the first organic molecule, acetic acid, which is basically vinegar, the show worked its way up to whales—or was planning to, anyway. I can't be certain. I fell asleep during the part about hagfishes.

Man, are those some ugly critters!

I regret falling asleep, because I would have liked to know how bad a whale's blowhole exhaust actually smells. Maybe they'll rerun the program someday. I just hope it's not during pledge week.

However, before falling asleep, I remember watching something about how fish are the most successful animals ever to have lived, the world's preeminent vertebrates, with a fossil history dating back nearly half a billion years. Today, the narrator explained, there are more than 24,000 species of fish, compared to only 4,000 mammal species.

Outnumbered six to one!

And if growing long whiskers is any indication of old age, some of the oldest kinds of fish around are catfish.

Defenseless lower species, my foot! I thought. *Cade's swimming up the wrong stream.*

A Fool and His Aroma

When the rosy fingertips of dawn nudged me awake on Sunday morning, the airy dream-thought fading from my consciousness was that if ever we required proof of a Divine Plan, we need only consider how perfectly the pungent tang of the first organic molecule (vinegar) complements the "fishy" taste of catfish.

With a side order of fried potatoes, it's alpha and omega, all in one.

Fish and chips.

Manna from heaven.

"Leigh Ann," my mother called from downstairs. "Cade's great-grandfather is here to see you."

No one expects a visit from the 107-year-old Earl Emerson Carlsen on a Sunday morning. Not the sad-eyed, stoop-shouldered preacher at the Pottersville Ecumenical Church, or the gabby freckled waitress at the Pottersville Country Corner Cafe, or the police-man behind the billboard in the Wal-Mart parking lot, and certainly not me, his neighbor, a fourteen-year-old girl who lives for the weekend because that's the only time I can sleep late.

"Do you mind if we speak outside?" the Carlsen patriarch asked, his voice as firm and commanding as that of a man half his age. "It's a matter requiring some discretion."

"I'm wearing pajamas," I said. "Hardly what I'd call discreet, no matter how far out in the country we may be."

"Perhaps Mr. Carlsen will be kind enough to wait in the kitchen while you change," my mother proposed. "I'll start coffee."

"How very kind of you," Mr. Carlsen replied, bowing in an old-world manner.

By the time I'd showered, brushed my teeth, slipped into jeans and a sweatshirt, and applied makeup and a spritz of Tommy Girl, it was apparent from the aromas rising up the staircase that my mother and Pottersville's oldest man were enjoying not only a cup of coffee but bacon, eggs, cinnamon rolls, and a spirited conversation.

"There she is," my mother declared, as if I'd stepped out onto a stage. "My, don't you smell nice!"

I shrugged. How a person smells seemed a risky subject given the present company.

"So why all the mystery?" I asked once we were on the porch.

"I didn't want to put you on the spot in front of your mother," Mr. Carlsen answered. "I was once a young person myself."

Given the senior Mr. Carlsen's present appearance, this required a great deal of imagination.

"I don't understand," I said.

"Mr. Glossup advises me that Cade disappeared for several hours yesterday in Springfield," he explained. "I was hoping you could tell me where he went."

27

I paused to consider the implications. Was Cade in trouble? Was I in trouble? Would my response to the senior Mr. Carlsen's interrogation get us into trouble? Was trouble just one of those things that was inevitable, given my lot in life? Are kids just destined to be in trouble all the time?

These are heady issues for which the answers are not readily forthcoming.

My discomfort was aggravated by the cold.

I should have put on a coat.

"I'm Cade's friend, not his bodyguard," I finally replied. "I'm sorry, but I don't know where he is or where he's been."

Technically speaking, this was a true statement. It would have passed muster in any court of law. Nevertheless, it was misleading, because, knowing about his recent goofball donation and his stupid bumper sticker tchotchke, I had a pretty good idea of where addle-brained, catfish-loving Cade might have wound up, given half a chance.

That stupid, smelly little weasel!

Words fail us all the time. But nowhere are we more at a loss for words than when describing odors. Even though each smell consists of a single molecule, as identifiable and precise as a musical note on a scale, when it comes to expressing an olfactory sensation, we become vague, as if no one else could have an identical experience.

We aren't so tentative when it comes to the other senses. Say "lime green" or "lemon yellow," and everybody nods. Or "rough as sandpaper," "smooth as silk," "warm as toast," or "slippery as an eel," and again there's a silent acknowledgment of understanding.

Sound has a complete, comprehensible vocabulary. Middle C, for example. But try to tell someone about an aroma wafting through an open window that's a combination of honey mustard and sweaty field mice and you get a blank, open-mouthed stare.

"Say what?" they reply.

Even famous perfumes baffle us. How does one describe Oscar? Or Chanel No. 5? Or Windsong? Or Shalimar? Or White Shoulders?

Sweet? Flowery? Citrusy? Earthy? Powdery?

Cade Carlsen had an unpleasant aroma all his own. And while it rivaled that of Norway rats crowded into a garbage can, as his friend, I was not about to rat him out.

Ever the optimist, I held out hope for our future.

The Chemical Curse of Mankind

Who knows what causes attraction between two people?

Some believe it to be appearance: wide cheekbones, a square jaw, dazzling blue-green eyes, a confident gait, a muscular torso.

Some say it's common interests, or simple proximity, or the scientific pull of opposites.

There are a few who claim that it's all based on desperation, on biological clocks, on the rebound effect, on the fear that this may be the last chance.

Still others put it down to smell.

Pheromones. Chemistry. Mingled molecules.

About which, more soon.

(Ah, I love your cologne! Marry me.)

Cade Carlsen was a complex case. At best, his body odor was confusing.

At its base was something resembling an expensive cedar-wrapped cigar burning in a marble ashtray. It included notes of newborn puppy, fresh sage, wild shitake mushroom, unopened paperback book, barbecued pork ribs, and patchouli bath soap, but the effect of this uniquely enticing foundation was ruined by a lifetime of contact with the nasty, gag-inducing aromatic signature of the family product, Stink City catfish bait, a smell that I shall hereafter refer to simply as Carlsenstink.

In the person of Cade Carlsen, I found myself both attracted and repelled at one and the same time—mostly repelled.

What the heart can't be sure of, the nose knows.

For me, it was a true dilemma.

Not so for Miss Martina Hyde. The only odor the founder of FISHTALE (the Foundation for Ichthyology Studies and Humane Treatment of Aquatic Life Everywhere) could detect was the smell of money. Thrilled with her luck when the goose had mailed her a golden egg, she became absolutely giddy when the fool himself showed up at her doorstep, declaring himself to be a willing pigeon.

"Do come in," she gasped, like a witch in the woods inviting lost children into a cottage made of gingerbread and candy.

"I'm here to redeem my family name," Cade explained.

"And so you shall," Miss Hyde replied. "May I offer you some refreshment?"

What followed may have looked like lemonade and sugar cookies but was, in fact, a witch's brew of hogwash and baloney. Among other things, the crafty old she-devil advised her gullible houseguest that the ancient Egyptians ("the most advanced civilization known to mankind," she declared) had worshiped catfish as being the earthly—or watery—embodiment of the gods.

"Are you sure?" Cade said. "I thought it was cats."

"A lot of people are confused by that one," Miss Hyde replied with a condescending chuckle. "It turns out that one of the stone tablets had gotten chipped and nobody noticed. But when the missing hieroglyphic was discovered years later filed away in a museum drawer in London where it had been mistakenly identified as a Pharaoh's cuff link, it became clear that what the ancient Egyptians were talking about was Nile River catfish."

"Holy smokes!" Cade exclaimed.

"Precisely," Miss Hyde responded. "That's why today you never see an Egyptian eating catfish."

"I can't say that I've ever seen an Egyptian eating anything," Cade said. "I don't think there are any Egyptians in Pottersville."

"And why would there be?" Miss Hyde observed.

"The town is practically wall-to-wall with catfish restaurants."

The conversation went on like this for much of the afternoon, with Miss Hyde's fish stories becoming increasingly outrageous, but poor Cade, so good-hearted, had long since left his common sense behind.

When the subject shifted from spurious history to his great-grandfather's vast fortune, he agreeably spilled the beans in detail to his malevolent interrogator.

"Basically," Cade concluded, "my great-grandfather gives me whatever I want. So I try not to be greedy."

"What a nice boy you are," the old woman managed to cough out while clutching at her heart, which was racing from excitement.

In his glass bowl a few feet away, Giorgio did a flip for joy.

Inside Miss Hyde's head an old but enduring song sprang forth: "We're in the money," it begins. And the second verse is the same as the first.

What can you say when two people get together for the wrong reasons? That they deserve each other? Not in Cade's case, I think, and not simply because he is my friend. No, Cade was overcome by something much more powerful than his naive, still-developing teenage brain could handle.

Perhaps it was Miss Hyde's flamboyance, her dramatic reactions to anything he said, her inventive, garrulous patter, her overwhelming presence, like an animal too big for its cage—such a contrast to the meek agreeability of Cade's grandparent-dominated parents.

And possibly it was pheromones.

Apparently, we are helpless against these.

Poor Cade.

Poor me.

Poor all of us.

The French Connection

Pheromones are mysterious, naturally occurring chemical attractants—special "invisible" body odors—about which much is known and little understood. But according to one scientist, the stuff is so potent that just one female moth's worth of pheromones can cause a trillion male moths to come a-courting, more or less against their will.

Pheromones. The odorless odor. The one that dogs can detect but humans can only react to. Like an invisible ray, or magical electromagnet, or mind control.

The powerful supersubstance is specific to each species, thank goodness, so humans don't have to worry about being bothered by, say, giraffes, or caterpillars, or canaries of the opposite sex attempting to mate with them. (The same can't always be said for dogs, because, as any dog owner knows, there are occasions when dogs will be dogs.)

Some experts speculate that pheromones are more than simply species-specialized, that they are the reason that we form likes and dislikes of certain people. They suggest that because of minute variations in pheromones, someone who makes one person do a flutter-dance of desire will have no effect whatsoever on a different person.

And all this time I thought it was based on personality.

If the scientists are right, then there's really no need to wear makeup or shave your legs. Whatever the reason for his attraction to the Springfield-based she-devil, Cade Carlsen left his meeting with Miss Hyde in thrall, like a goofy lover carrying a torch, and, as the world was eventually to find out, carrying an evil secret assignment, as well.

Which brings me to literary history.

In the short history of smell, it's a pivotal, world-famous event: One afternoon, a Frenchman soaked some cake crumbs in his tea. When he lifted the spoon to his mouth, his past suddenly sprang to life before his eyes.

Triggered by a taste, which was created by a smell, whole portions of the man's long-forgotten childhood were recalled in vivid detail. The time was the early 1900s. The man's name was Marcel Proust. The result of his experience was a series of books called *Remembrance of Things Past* by some and *In Search of Lost Time* by others, an ambiguity that apparently depends on how one chooses to translate French into English.

I mention that famous episode because shortly after his clandestine mission to Springfield, about which he remained maddenly mum, Cade and I attempted a similar experiment ourselves in his family's library, with mixed results.

Not having access to the particular type of teacake that Marcel Proust enjoyed—a little shell-shaped sponge cake called a madeleine—we used Hostess

Twinkies from Quik-Trip. And since neither of us cared much for hot tea, we substituted a Wild Cherry Pepsi with ice.

Cade went first, dipping his Twinkie into his cold drink, taking a bite, then closing his eyes to try to visualize some meaningful event from his childhood.

"What do you remember?" I asked eagerly.

As if in a trance, he replied, "I remember falling off my bicycle."

"That was last November," I said. "You broke your arm. Your cast with everybody's signatures is still on your bookshelf. How could you *not* remember something like that?"

Cade seemed to think he had failed me. Deferring to my superior knowledge, he suggested, "Maybe you should try it."

Dipping the blunt end of the Twinkie into the still-fizzing drink, I took a bite. It was a particularly fresh Twinkie, I thought, so I took another bite, after which, unfortunately, it was all gone.

"Well, Leigh Ann?" Cade asked.

"I think they're making Twinkies smaller," I observed. "It's a sneaky way they have of raising the price. Let me try another one."

This time I took a smaller bite. All of a sudden, in

my mind's eye, I saw a scene from when I couldn't have been more than four years old. I was sitting on a rough plank pier with a pink Barbie fishing pole in my hands, my legs dangling over the water. I could actually see the water sparkling in the summer sun, as if I were right there, with the cork bobbing in and out of the sparkles.

My father was sitting beside me. Between us was a metal bucket in which a catfish about the size of a chili dog swam in lazy circles. I could smell the rich rot of thick algae in the lake, the wild onions growing on the hillside, the sweet blue smoke from my father's cigar.

My father took a swig of Wild Cherry Pepsi from a two-liter bottle, then passed the drink to me. It was warm and flat, but the sensation that ran through my body then, and once again as I now recalled the moment, made me shudder.

Marcel Proust was on to something. Taste and smell can take you places. You can even visit people who have died.

"Well?" Cade repeated. "Anything?"

I stared at the rug, my heart on the knife edge of grief.

"I remember when you broke your arm," I told him.

Cade nodded and looked out the window, where a robin was fighting to extract a fat worm from the soil beneath a leafless hickory tree.

Once again, spring was attempting to gain a foothold in Pottersville.

A Girl, a Plan, Springfield

"I ran into your great-grandfather the other day," I announced. "That is one wrinkled old man."

This was not simply idle conversation, but an effort to get Cade to confide in me. As well known as he was throughout the world because of his unusually advanced age, Earl Emerson Carlsen was not a common sight among the townspeople of Pottersville. Some suspected he avoided the locals because of his elevated financial position.

I knew better.

Just imagine how much a 107-year-old man who's lived most of his life in tiny Pottersville has seen of his hometown. If you live long enough, you eventually reach a point where your curiosity about most things becomes satisfied. Spring. Summer. Winter. Fall. Been there. Done that.

Neighbor A. Neighbor B. Neighbor C. Heard all their stories several times over. Wasn't that interested the first time. I think I'll just read a magazine instead.

Should you ever deign to enter the Carlsen home, you are likely to find Cade's great-grandfather in his study just off the living room, reading a book or a fishing magazine, or dozing on his cream-colored leather couch.

Sometimes he will be giving instructions about the operation of the bait business to a member of the family, most often his browbeaten son, Cade's father, Lenny, who smells the worst of all of them.

This brings me to two important points: one, that one of the reasons smell is such an underappreciated sense is because we are socially conditioned to be ashamed of many of the smells our bodies inevitably make; and two, if you are fortunate enough to be born into a thriving business, there are some things you just have to put up with. After a while you don't notice the stink.

This dulling of the senses may not be limited to bad odors, in fact. It may also apply to such things as killing for sport, eating the flesh of other creatures, and treating people as if they're not worth a tinker's damn. If you engage in something long enough, no matter how out of the ordinary it actually is, it begins to feel normal. Ask anybody who's been to war.

Or consider the example of history's most egregious tyrants. To them, their horrible deeds were just another day at the office.

Consider as well the example of my occasionally blocked sinuses. Even when they were partially clear, which wasn't often, I could tolerate being inside the Carlsens' singularly odiferous house.

Familiarity with a situation is also why, while Cade and I were engaged in conversation, I no longer gave any thought to his great-grandfather's quietly reading the latest issue of *Catfish In-sider* on the other side of the bathroom door, listening to every word I said.

Out of sight, out of mind.

Just another day at the Carlsens'.

"He came to my house to pump me for information about what you're up to," I explained to Cade. "But don't worry. I outsmarted him."

"Maybe," Cade replied. "But you can't reveal what you don't know."

"You got me there," I agreed.

"Anyway," Cade went on, proving he's not the sharpest knife in the drawer, "it's not like you'd want to help me make a dramatic public statement during the annual Springfield Catfish Derby. It's just not your thing, Leigh Ann. Besides, how would you get there? Springfield is a hundred miles away."

A dramatic public statement?

So that's it! I thought. *The little stinker thinks he can make a difference by giving a speech to a bunch of country rubes in bass boats?*

What a doofus!

This boy definitely needed my help.

Few plans arrive in the mind fully formed. History teaches that whether it's waging war, making peace, running a business, or raising a family, you start with some sort of fuzzy goal and a few sketchy ideas about how to achieve it, and all the rest—the details—you simply make up as you go along.

My plan was to shadow Cade and try to save his wrong-headed butt (or is it wrong-butted head?) from himself. To accomplish this, I figured I'd better get myself invited to the three-day catfish caper in Springfield.

To compete in the fishing tournament required a

$250 entry fee, plus a bunch of fishing equipment, such as a bass boat, for instance, that I didn't have. So entering that part of the contest was out of the question, financially speaking. My mother and I ate enough macaroni and cheese as it was.

I thought about signing on with one of the event vendors, flipping burgers, or chopping cabbage for coleslaw, or selling souvenir T-shirts, or supervising the skee-ball games, but in this state you're supposed to be at least sixteen years old to hold a job.

Then I remembered about Cade's great-grandfather being selected the tournament's very first King Catfish. Now that he and I were better acquainted, I reasoned, maybe I could persuade him to use his influence to get me named Queen Catfish.

Well, look at it this way. It was worth a try.

A Helping Paw

Queen Catfish.

It had a certain ring to it, I had to admit.

Such an accolade would be embarrassing at Pottersville High School, of course, but not any more embarrassing than having a stinkpot for a sidekick.

But since I knew hardly anybody in Springfield and the event lasted only three days, I figured I could handle the publicity.

After that, whatever ridicule the kids at school chose to extend my way would quickly subside as they moved on to somebody else's screwed-up, sad-sack, disadvantaged life to make fun of.

Certainly, around Pottersville, there was no shortage of choices.

I was definitely qualified for the royal position. I knew how to sit with my knees together, how to stand, wave, and smile, and I enjoyed eating catfish as much as anybody—lots more than one weird person I could name.

Since Cade had to work all day Saturday filling jars for the family business, I chose that afternoon to call on his great-grandfather.

"Why, hello there, Leigh Ann, honey," Lani Carlsen, Cade's plump, red-faced, sweaty, and naturally friendly mother greeted me, opening the screen door. "Why don't you come on inside and set yourself down a spell? I've got a pitcher of fresh-made sun tea and I might just be able to rustle up some cinnamon rolls."

"That's okay," I told her. "I'll just wait out

44

on the porch for Mr. Carlsen, if you don't mind."

I sat down in a white wicker rocker and watched a groundhog shuffling around in a patch of tulips. Overhead, a hawk circled in profound disappointment, wishing that his talons were larger or that the groundhog he could see so clearly weren't so obviously obese.

From out of nowhere, a pack of dogs showed up and chased the clumsy groundhog into his underground hideout. One of the pursuers, a brown and tan dappled dachshund puppy with long, floppy ears, tried to follow the gopher into the ground, where the little dog immediately got his oversize head stuck.

The puppy's muffled howls tore at my hardened heart. Not to mention that even when it's been halfway down a varmint hole nothing smells quite so nice as a new puppy.

Which was how it came to be that when the screen door slapped shut at the Carlsen house and Cade's great-grandfather stepped onto the porch, saying, "I understand you want to speak to me," I was clutching the wriggling little animal to my chest and singing softly, "And if that diamond ring don't shine, Mama's gonna buy you a five-and-dime."

"Well, your life has changed forever," Earl Emerson Carlsen observed.

"He needed me," I replied.

"That's how it happens," Mr. Carlsen said. "He's part of a group that showed up a few days ago. I've been trying to take care of them, but they're a lot of work. Do you want him?"

I didn't even have to reply with words. My eyes grew big, I hugged the puppy tightly, the puppy wagged his tail like a butterfly beating its wings, and the deal was sealed in an unspoken second.

"Now, what else can I do?" Mr. Carlsen asked.

I told him about my desire to keep an eye on Cade in Springfield during the fishing tournament.

"I'm worried about the boy," I explained in my most mature voice.

To my surprise, Mr. Carlsen seemed interested in helping me.

"I can't pull as many strings as I once could," he confessed. "As I'm sure you can appreciate, at my age most of my colleagues have passed away, many of them before you were born. But Stink City is a major exhibitor at the Catfish Derby, so I'm sure I can work out something—even if it means I have to outsmart somebody."

With that last phrase he gave me a wink.

Hmm, I wondered, caught off-guard by the old man's choice of words. *Is it possible that he heard me talking to Cade?*

I shook Mr. Carlsen's hand and thanked him for both the puppy and his help with my plan. His hand felt like crumpled sandpaper.

At first, shadowing Cade was no different from not shadowing Cade. We walked to the bus stop together in the morning, we had lunch together in the school cafeteria, and we walked home together, after which Cade had to go to work and I had responsibilities to my new dog, among which was giving him a name, a matter of no small importance.

Names matter.

Cade, for example, is a cool name, even if the kid it belongs to is not.

Some names, to put it mildly, stink. I've mentioned some of the more repellant names given to various species of fish. But even within a species it's just as awful. Catfish, for example, are condemned to bear names like bullhead, madtom, hardhead, flathead, and widemouth. With monikers like these, is it any wonder that few people care about their feelings?

So that's why I was so careful in selecting a name

for my new little dog. This and the fact that his head was fully one fourth of his total length and his nose at least half of that.

Nosey.

It's a look. It's an attitude. It's a way of life.

It's my dog.

An Ominous Warning

A problem arose on the school bus. The driver, a red-faced country woman named Nipsy-Dale Dood, advised Cade that since he'd begun working in the family factory again, he was no longer welcome to ride with the other students. Not that it mattered to her, Nipsy-Dale Dood claimed—she'd smelled worse coming from her barn—but there'd been complaints from others, and she was simply following orders from the higher-ups.

"My hands are tied," the bus driver explained.

"Then I'd be extra careful on the curves," I suggested, picking up my backpack from the front seat and joining my neighbor by the side of the road.

"Now what?" he asked.

"We could walk to school," I said.

"By the time we got there it'd be over," Cade replied.

Although it was still early, the day was already beautiful, with clear skies and the temperature headed for the low eighties for the first time in many months. The only problem was the wind, which gusted across the pasture, picking up the dusty residue of winter.

Following a single, loud sneeze, my sinuses filled up and my sense of smell shut down.

"Bless you," Cade said.

"Thank you," I replied, sniffing. "I mean that."

Leaving our backpacks beneath a bee tree, we set out walking with no particular destination in mind. We passed the place where the hippie woman, reputed to be a Wiccan, raised rabbits and goats, and the house belonging to the Irish family with five kids under the age of seven.

At the tumbledown hay barn, Cade and I picked daffodils. I could hear the boards creaking as the sun caused the rotted barn wood to expand and pop its nails.

Stepping over a rusted barbed-wire fence, we left the populated world behind. In the distance, across a forgotten field of dandelions and scattered tufts of grass, flanked by wild fruit trees on the very cusp of bloom, was a small stream-fed lake with a waterfall no higher than the countertop in the Pottersville Country Corner Cafe.

The little lake had once been a watering hole for expensive show horses, but in more recent years only migrating waterfowl and the steady parade of homeless dogs looking for the Carlsen place took advantage of its riches.

"It's almost warm enough to swim," Cade observed.

"I didn't bring a suit," I pointed out.

"Are you wearing underwear?" he asked.

"Why, Cade Carlsen!" I exclaimed. "That's for me to know."

"And for me to find out," he said, breaking into a run. "Last one in is a rotten egg."

No, Cade, I thought to myself, considering the awful sulfuric odor a rotten egg puts off. *That's a distinction you'll always have over me.*

Sploosh!

Maybe fish don't have it as bad as some people say. Once my teeth stopped chattering, I kicked my legs and glided underneath the surface of the pond as if the water were my home. Submerged, I could neither see nor hear nor smell, but none of this mattered. The feeling against my skin was everything.

Imagine what it must be like to have the rivers as your natural home. Unlike those of us confined by gravity and atmosphere and odd body shape to a two-dimensional world, for the creatures of the water, up, down, back, forth, this way, that way, whichever way you choose to go, you can.

In the water, the world seems endless.

Afterward, Cade and I lay on our backs on the bank, drying our skivvies in the sun. High above us, wisps of lazy clouds glided over in atmospheric imitation of fish, an observation that I shared with Cade.

"A lot of people are going to start paying attention to fish," he said, adding ominously, "just you wait."

"What are you saying, Cade?" I asked, turning my back to him while slipping into my shirt.

"What I'm saying," he continued, as if he—or someone he'd been talking to—had given the matter a lot of thought, "is that the only way social change comes about is through violent revolution."

"Oh, good grief!" I exclaimed. "What nonsense! Surely you don't believe that."

The day, it seemed, had taken a sudden turn for the worse.

"The Founding Fathers went to war to make future generations free," Cade recited robotically. "Why shouldn't somebody do the same for fish?"

Sniffing through my blocked sinuses, I let out a long, desperate sigh.

"There are so many obvious answers to that one that I wouldn't know where to begin," I told him, standing up and pulling on my jeans. Never easy to do elegantly, it was especially difficult with wet legs.

"Keep your back turned, freak," I warned him.

How seriously should one take talk of extremism in defense of invertebrates coming from a boy wearing wet plaid boxer shorts two sizes too large?

"Anyway," I added, unable to disguise my annoyance, "I have to get back to my dog."

"Okay, Leigh Ann," Cade mumbled, equally miffed at my unsympathetic reaction. "But don't say I didn't warn you."

Shadowing Cade Carlsen

Cade Carlsen's parents resolved the school transportation issue not by driving Cade to school themselves—they were much too busy in the bait factory for that—but by persuading Cade's great-grandfather to pay for the school district to get a second school bus and an additional bus driver, a man who identified himself as Gucci.

Consequently, I had to choose between my more or less normal-smelling schoolmates and my aromatically repulsive neighbor. At the time, my concern for Cade's state of mind trumped my inclination for an ordinary life.

"Hey, Leigh Ann," he greeted me, as the bus skidded to a stop.

"Today let's just ride without talking, shall we?" I suggested.

I was still annoyed by Cade's crazy thinking.

Meanwhile, in Springfield, the executive director of FISHTALE (the Foundation for Ichthyology Studies and Humane Treatment of Aquatic Life Everywhere) was also concerned with transportation, having spent her weekend shopping for a new car, certain that her pigeon was coming home to roost, her ship was coming in, and she'd managed to capture a leprechaun.

A red one would be nice, she thought, *but gold is attractive, too.*

One thing Miss Martina Hyde was sure of was

that her next automobile must be European. After all, she reminded herself, from her mother's side, there coursed through her visible purple veins a pint or more of fine French blood. This, perhaps, explained why Miss Hyde bathed so infrequently, preferring to dust her sagging body with scented powder instead.

"You know," the salesman said, continuing to hold his nose after returning to the dealership from an abbreviated test drive, "you really ought to consider a convertible."

"You think so?" Miss Hyde responded.

"Goodness, yes," the salesman replied. "A woman such as yourself requires an open car."

Or a complete fumigation, he fought off the urge to add.

"What a flatterer you are," Miss Hyde said with girlish pleasure. "I would look good in a convertible, wouldn't I?"

The salesman merely coughed.

Back in Pottersville, Cade's parents began yet another day laboring without complaint in the bait factory, mixing revolting substances in vats and screwing tops on plastic jars, secure in the knowledge that someday they would inherit all that they beheld.

That Stink City's founder and sole proprietor had managed to hold on beyond the astonishing human age of one hundred and seven years was discouraging, they admitted, but eventually, they kept reminding themselves, their day would surely come, and for when it did they had lots of ideas for expanding the company.

"Fishing hats," Lenny Carlsen said. "Stink City all-weather fishing hats. All fishermen need hats. The sun can kill you."

"And snack foods," his wife, Lani, added. "Stink City Sweet and Salty Snacks. You can't keep on fishing if you're hungry."

"You can if what you're hungry for is fish," Lenny disagreed.

"Well, except for that, of course," Lani responded, never one to linger in an argument with her husband. Besides, she was smart enough to recognize that she had not been born into the pending fortune; she had married into it.

In fact, if it weren't for being matrimonially attached to Lenny's birthright, she might have ended up as one of those old ladies on the rural routes surrounding Pottersville who sell used clothes and broken-down appliances from their front porches. Or worse: who pitch such things into ravines, ditches, creeks, ponds, and lakes.

With dreams in their heads of an empire soon to come, the Carlsen couple dutifully stirred and poured and packaged up the family stench, while in the house, from the comfort of his study, Cade's great-grandfather sat on his cream-colored leather sofa and thumbed through the pages of *Springfield* magazine ("Your monthly peek at everything from chickens to chic") and made a phone call that would change my life.

Ignorant of all of this at the time, I gazed out the window of Cade's personal school bus as it bounced in and out of potholes scattered like lunar craters along the gravel road, trying to remember last night's dream. It had something to do with a major disaster in Springfield. The Mud Lake dam had been blown up by bearded, turban-wearing Middle Eastern terrorists. Thousands perished in the flood.

I remembered my mother being there, and Cade's great-grandfather, and my little dog, Nosey. I remembered holding him against my face.

How frightened I was!

How soft Nosey was!

Why is it that when we dream, I wondered, we can't smell what's happening?

You can see a dream in living color. You can hear dialogue, music, all sorts of sounds—just like in a movie. You can feel temperature and touch, even the soft, warm moisture of a kiss. But for some reason in a dream you can't detect odors, not that I can ever recall, which is ironic, since smell and taste and memory are inextricably connected deep inside our brains.

Thanks to Gucci missing the turn at the junction of highways M and KK, Cade and I were an hour late for school.

"You'd think they'd train these people," I muttered to Cade about the choice of Gucci, "before turning them loose on normal society."

As things turned out, it was the wrong day to be tardy.

Modern Science

Our tardiness was especially unfortunate, because, as it happened, an all-school assembly was under way, about which I'd completely forgotten. Two lecturers from out of town had been scheduled, and I'd already missed most of the first one, B. F. Skinner, an elderly and frail Harvard psychologist, who was wrapping up his presentation called "I Smell a Rat," in which he claimed to be able to recognize six hundred and some odd individual laboratory rats by their distinctive, individual aromas.

"Big Charles smelled like tooth decay, worm guts, and ripe Camembert cheese," he reminisced. "His firstborn son, Charles Junior, smelled like week-old cat litter."

And so on.

Dang! I thought. *What a day to show up late! This guy's really interesting.*

At least I hadn't missed the main event, Linda Buck, a middle-aged lady with a shag haircut and pleasant smile, who, with her colleague, Richard Axel, had won the Nobel Prize for Physiology or Medicine in 2004 for their investigations into how our genes, noses, and brains all work together to detect odors.

"It's great to be here in Pottersville," Linda Buck shouted into the microphone, which responded with a shriek of electronic feedback. "Is there anybody out there from Las Vegas?"

Except for the usual coughing, throat clearing, nose blowing, muttering, and shuffling of feet, the room was quiet.

"How about L.A.?" Linda Buck cried, again trying to connect with the listless crowd the way she'd seen it done on TV by entertainers working crowds in big cities. "New York? Chicago? Nobody? What about Little Rock? Paragould? Pine Bluff? West Plains? Is there anybody here from Thayer?"

As happens in every assembly at Pottersville High School, Lance Boyle, fast asleep, tumbled out of his chair.

"Has anybody ever *been* to one of those places? Come on, give me a show of hands," Linda Buck pleaded.

Coach Tucker stood up.

"I drove past the exit to Mountain Home once, but it was a long time ago, and to tell the truth, I was lost," he said.

The audience tittered at Coach Tucker's revelation, because by "lost" they knew that Coach Tucker actually meant "drunk." That's why nobody ever rode with him.

"Hmm," Linda Buck responded. "Well, so be it. Let's get started."

Linda Buck is a person who knows a lot about the sense of smell.

"Each of us is capable of detecting about ten thousand different odors," she announced.

Still hopeful of establishing rapport with the kids of Pottersville High School, she tried a method she'd seen used by a standup comedian on Comedy Central, adding with tongue in cheek, "And without a doubt, one of them is this high school."

Too long, in my opinion, the Nobel laureate waited for the laugh that never came.

For a brainy, sophisticated out-of-towner, Pottersville High will always be a tough crowd. Instead of Linda Buck, the administration might have considered inviting Cooter from *The Dukes of Hazzard*, or possibly Grampa Munster.

"Okay, but here's the thing," Linda Buck labored intrepidly on. "We've identified only about three hundred and fifty olfactory receptors in our noses, so how is it that we can smell ten thousand different things?"

A hand went up in the third row. It belonged to Missy Rumpole, the school know-it-all.

"You missed some receptors when you were

counting?" Missy said, in that way she has of making everything sound like a question.

Linda Buck smiled, not from pleasure, I gathered, but from what might have been either a moment of gastric distress or an instant dislike of Missy Rumpole, who has been known to elicit both effects from all kinds of people.

"We didn't miss any, I assure you," the celebrated scientist declared, openly irritated with Missy Rumpole, with the students and faculty of Pottersville High School, and not to mention with her dumb cluck of a booking agent back in Boston, whom she vowed to fire the moment she could get to her cell phone.

"In mice we've found a thousand such receptors," Linda Buck explained, "and mice have smaller noses, as perhaps you've noticed—quite a bit smaller than yours, my dear."

Ha! I thought. *That put her in her place.* Missy Rumpole's got a honker like a toucan.

"The reason," Linda Buck went on, "has to do with the number of unique combinations formed among—"

Missy's hand shot up again.

"Yes?" Linda Buck said, now even more peeved than before.

"Did you really win the Nobel Prize?" Missy asked.

"Richard Axel and I did," Linda Buck stated smugly.

"So he helped you?" Missy clarified. "You didn't do it by yourself? At our school, we do our own science projects, you know? It's, like, a rule?"

"Well, that's all the time we have for questions," Linda Buck announced.

But the big news was yet to come.

The Secret of Life, Interrupted

It's too bad Missy Rumpole and Linda Buck didn't hit it off, because I have a feeling that if they had we'd all be living much longer lives.

Oh, well.

That's the way it is with girls sometimes.

"I was hoping to tell you about an exciting new project," an obviously out-of-sorts Linda Buck announced by way of meting out group punishment. "Our laboratory's extraordinary success with the mechanisms of smell has led us to search for the mechanisms of aging and the human life span. Currently, we're screening for chemicals that extend the life span of nematodes. Can these chemicals extend human life as well?"

Coach Tucker tentatively raised his hand, but Linda Buck had had enough of him, too. Besides, didn't the poor Neanderthal know that it was a rhetorical question?

"You won't be hearing any more about it from me—ever," Linda Buck promised, "but perhaps you'll read the answer in your newspaper someday. That is, if you *have* a newspaper in Pottersville."

Missy Rumpole's arm shot up yet again, with one hand on her opposite elbow, pushing her arm higher as she strained to get Linda Buck's attention. As everyone at Pottersville High School knew, Missy Rumpole's uncle Morris was the circulation director for the *Pottersville Post.*

But Linda Buck had had it with all of these people. Waving a dismissive goodbye to the audience, the famous scientist hurried off the stage.

"Lord, deliver me," Miss Froth heard Linda Buck say as she sprinted to her waiting limousine.

"Well, at least she's a religious person," Miss

Froth subsequently reported to her academic colleagues during the group gossip session in the teachers' lounge.

"That was a big waste of time," Cade complained as we shuffled down the hall with the other kids heading for the cafeteria.

"I just wish that Missy Rumpole had kept her mouth shut," I responded. "I would have liked to know more about the nematode thing—like, for instance, what *is* a nematode?"

"It's a kind of worm," Cade said.

"How do you know that?" I asked in surprise.

It's not often Cade Carlsen knows something I don't.

"I was on the front porch one day when my great-grandfather received a sealed bucketful of them from a laboratory in North Carolina," Cade explained. "They're small, they're cheap, they're plentiful, and they grow fast, so they're used in research all the time," he told me.

"Why would your great-grandfather need research worms?" I asked, surprised to see that Chef Ludd had put processed cheese sauce on the gruel for the second day in a row. "Didn't we just have this?" I added.

64

"Yesterday," he advised. "But I had a package of coconut-sprinkled Sno Balls instead. They were excellent, especially the pink one. As for the nematodes, I have no idea what my great-grandfather does with them. But since they're worms, I figure it must have something to do with fishing. In case nobody ever told you, Leigh Ann, fish enjoy eating worms."

"Oh," I said, deciding to take another chance on the gruel with cheese sauce in order to save my quarters for the journey to my coronation in Springfield. "Well, that makes sense."

This time, spring was taking no chances. Instead of making a tentative feint, it exploded in Pottersville like a flower bomb, with everything blooming at once—the huge pink tulip trees, the wiry yellow forsythia, the delicate redbuds, dogwoods, and feathery mimosa trees, the orchards of cherry trees, peach trees, apples, persimmons, and pears. The landscape was reborn with pastel colors, and as a consequence I could hardly breathe.

The fishing season, too, shifted into high gear, with the highways on Saturdays clogged not just with the Amish sitting ramrod-straight in horse-drawn buggies going about their regular Saturday marketing, but with bleary-eyed, beer-drinking hillbillies in baseball caps crammed three abreast into the cabs of huge pickup trucks pulling even bigger boat trailers.

The *Pottersville Post* reported catfish eagerly taking minnows, night crawlers, cutbait, chicken livers, shad sides, cheese doodles, spoons, and jigs, with a near-record catfish near Searcy (nineteen pounds) hitting a doubled-up strip of lightly breaded fried bologna.

Over at the Carlsen house, the factory was humming day and night. Twice in the same week, Cade never even showed up at school.

"Aren't you worried about your grades?" I asked him, during a moment when Gucci had stopped by the side of the road to consult a plastic-coated highway map he'd bought for five dollars at Quik-Trip.

"I'm worried about a lot of things," Cade replied. "But after next month, my worries will be over."

Now what is that supposed to mean? I wondered.

You May Already Be a Winner

" . . . my worries will be over."

No sooner had Cade uttered these unnerving words than a brand-new bright red BMW Z4

Roadster roared past, its chrome wheels spitting gravel against the school bus, and, soon afterward, running the hapless Amish farmer off the road into a weed-filled, trash-laden, snake-infested ditch.

"Imbecille!" Gucci shouted in Italian out the window, shaking his hairy fist.

The driver downshifted to negotiate a curve, and as the flashy convertible slowed, I saw on its back bumper a sticker bearing the following familiar phrase:

FISH FEEL PAIN®, it read.

Miss Martina Hyde, I realized. *The devil's hand-maiden expands her sphere of influence.*

Strangely, Cade seemed unfazed. Perhaps he didn't notice. It all happened so fast.

The following Saturday, while Cade was working, I was in the front yard, watering the vegetable patch and watching Nosey try to bury a pork bone, when Debra Dogwald, the Pottersville postmistress, pulled up in her squat government truck.

"Is your mom home?" Debra called without getting out of the truck.

"She's inside," I told her. "Keep an eye on my dog, will you, and I'll go fetch her."

But Nosey was too preoccupied with rolling in a

spot of newfound stink to require federal supervision.

As it turned out, Debra Dogwald was delivering an official-looking letter with a stuck-on card that required my mother's signature.

"Who's it from?" I asked.

"The Greater Springfield Invitational Catfish Derby Organizing Committee," my mother read aloud.

"Why would they be writing to you?" I inquired.

"Let's find out, shall we?" she replied cheerfully, opening the envelope with a well-manicured but unpainted fingernail, and a moment later adding, "Well, now, that's odd."

"What's odd?" I asked, as Nosey continued to roll ecstatically on his elastic little back in the yard.

"They're thanking me for the application for my daughter, Miss Leigh Ann Moore, and are pleased to advise me that she—you—are among the five semi-finalists," my mother summarized. "They've enclosed certificates for three nights' lodging at the Fisherman's Inn and vouchers for meals at the Crazy Cajun Catfish Cafe. All we have to do is show up at the judge's stand at ten o'clock on May sixteenth, with you ready to perform."

She tapped her hand against the letter.

"An expense-paid trip to Springfield?" my mother mused. "It makes no sense. I've had no contact with these people. Maybe Debra got the wrong address."

"It can't be the wrong address," I observed. "Not if the letter mentions my name."

"You're right," my mother concurred. "Well, this is truly a mystery."

Nosey, having decided to share his recent success, was now rolling back and forth over my feet, wiping a thick, dark, odiferous substance on my once white tennis shoes, as if he were a sidewalk shoeshine man applying Kiwi polish.

"It's not as mysterious as you think," I confessed. "I'm guessing Cade's great-grandfather is behind this."

"Earl?" my mother said. "Why would Earl Emerson Carlsen do such a thing?"

"Because he's got lots of money and powerful connections," I replied. "Not to mention, he likes you. Pulling strings is how rich people make friends."

"Pulling strings is how puppeteers make puppets dance," my mother replied ominously. "But under the circumstances, it is kind of sweet. I suppose a few days in Springfield could be fun. But even with a free room and meals, we're still going to need some spending money."

By now, thanks to Nosey, my tennis shoes were a putrid disaster. I'd probably wind up throwing them away. Only one other thing troubled me.

What, I wondered, did the letter mean by "ready to perform"?

Then I realized that it had to mean performing the duties of a queen.

Well, heck, I thought to myself. *That's easy. I was born to do that.*

Missy Rumpole must have complained to her uncle, and her uncle must have put a bug in the managing editor's ear, because one morning on the way to school, as I was skimming through Gucci's rumpled copy of the *Pottersville Post,* my eye paused at the editorial headline "Seeker of Fountain of Youth Passes Through Pottersville."

Although it got her name wrong, referring to her as Linda Bock instead of Linda Buck, the item opined that the recent appearance at the high school of "the prominent nose specialist and winner of one half of a Nobel Prize from some previous year" was evidence of "Pottersville's growing reputation as a hotbed for the exchange of controversial ideas."

Hmm, I thought. *That's one way of looking at it.*

In the next paragraph it went on: "When Miss Bock [sic] is not traveling to international cities soliciting funds for what some have dubbed 'nutball' research, the temperamental celebrity-scientist is busy sniffing for life-extending potions among the tiny bodies of living nematodes.

"All life, of course," the editor opined, "even that of the lowly nematodes, is precious."

"Hey, Cade," I said, nudging the silent boy sitting next to me. "Here's a guy you definitely should send a bumper sticker to."

A Better Life Through Chemistry

"In her peculiar endeavor involving longevity through nematode research," Linda Buck reminds the *Pottersville Post* of the Spanish explorer Juan Ponce de León, who in the sixteenth century scoured Florida in vain to locate the Fountain of Youth, a legendary stream with waters re-puted to prevent a person from dying of old age.

The *Pottersville Post* readers familiar with history may recall that Ponce de León not only was unsuccessful in his search but was killed by more established and possibly more knowledgeable Native Americans.

"There are lessons to be learned from this, the *Pottersville Post* believes."

Thus blabs the editorial.

I didn't think Linda Buck was all that temperamental, given the circumstances, but no doubt Missy was still upset about the verbal jab to her nose.

The newspaper's unsigned opinion concluded with the suggestion that "instead of wasting her time opening cans of worms in search of some magic potion, perhaps Miss Bock [sic] would be better served if she'd simply find out what Pottersville's most famous senior citizen, the 107-year-old Earl Emerson Carlsen, has for breakfast."

"At my house, it was bacon and eggs," I said.

"What was bacon and eggs?" Cade asked.

"Oh, it's just something in the newspaper about your great-grandfather," I replied. "It says scientists should learn what he has for breakfast."

"Post Raisin Bran," Cade said. "But I wish the media would leave him alone. They make my great-grandfather sound like some kind of freak. It's not his fault that he's old."

"True enough," I agreed. "He and the Planet Earth just have good chemistry."

"Ohhhh," Cade moaned. "Don't remind me of chemistry."

I'd forgotten that Cade was failing chemistry, although it wasn't entirely his fault. What with the long hours he'd been putting in at the bait factory, his sleeping late, his skipping school, and Gucci's getting lost all the time, first hour chemistry class at Pottersville High School had become for Cade one of those aggravating issues for which a person has to decide whether to fish or cut bait.

As his officially designated shadow, I urged him to give it one more try.

"Here's the deal in a walnut shell, Cade," I told him. "Chemistry is the key to understanding life. When push comes to shove, everything is molecular."

"Doesn't that suggest that biology is the more important science?" he responded.

"Don't argue with me, Cade," I warned him. "Let me remind you that I'm not the one who's failing here. You are."

Personally, I liked chemistry. I found it every bit as interesting as biology, while having all the predictability of mathematics.

Every atom has a number, and, consequently, when atoms combine to form molecules, they have numbers, too. So if you know what numbers you started with, when you mix different atoms together, you know what you're going to get.

No surprises. A predictable outcome. An orderly world.

Take acetic acid, for example, the vinegary-smelling stuff that scientists tell us is the original organic molecule. It's a simple combination of our planet's most common elements—carbon, hydrogen, and oxygen—and in chemistry is written down as CH_3CO_2H. Diluted with water, CH_3CO_2H is useful for cleaning floors, pickling cucumbers, and making coleslaw, as well as being the foundation for every single thing that lives.

How could someone not find this interesting? I wondered.

"The trouble with you, Cade," I told him, "is that you fail to comprehend the big picture."

"And what big picture is that?" he responded.

"The one that shows how everything in creation fits together," I replied. "How opposites not only attract but can't wait to get together to make something new."

"My stars, Leigh Ann," Cade said, waving his arms. "What on earth are you driving at? Romance?"

At that moment Gucci hit a major pothole, possibly something created overnight by the impact of a meteor, which caused the bus to lurch onto the shoulder before returning to the rutted road. The swerve knocked Cade off balance, and he landed in my lap. As usual, his body stunk of catfish bait, but his hair smelled like the vast, wide-open sea.

"I'm trying to talk to you about passing chemistry," I clarified, pushing his muscular body off me.

Among the many facts this blond-haired dullard failed to appreciate was that in chemistry, as perhaps in all things in life, it takes a measurable dose of bad to make things good.

According to those in the know, all the famous, exotic perfumes of the world, the ones that people spend fortunes to wear, contain at least one ingredient that by itself would make us puke like sick dogs. Consider these examples: a substance harvested from the rear ends of Chinese civet cats—no kidding— or that rare essence called ambergris, which whalers prized for centuries and remains in demand among the great perfumers of today. Ambergris is basically just a lump of petrified whale poop.

I could go on, but why disgust ourselves further? The point is made. Good smells contain bad smells. It takes two to tango. Opposites attract.

"By the way," Cade announced as we disembarked. "You may want to ride the other bus this afternoon. I'm getting picked up after school."

"Oh?" I said. "By whom?"

"No one you'd know," he replied enigmatically. "Just a friend."

Casing the Joint

Cade Carlsen's "friend," I learned, who was picking him up at school, was a flashy, fish-faced woman in a red convertible with a bumper sticker that read FISH FEEL PAIN®—the founder and executive director of FISHTALE (the Foundation for Ichthyology Studies and Humane Treatment of Aquatic Life Everywhere), that fraudulent, fish-obsessed, and possibly evil fruitcake named Miss Martina Hyde.

It was pretty clear their destination wasn't Cade's house. In fact (and I know because I timed it), it was three hours and nineteen minutes before that craven, cackling, conniving cradle robber brought my neighbor home.

"Where've you been?" I demanded, my eyes shooting sparks, my teeth bared, my throat breathing dragon fire.

Poor Nosey, thinking that my onset of fury was his fault, hid terrified underneath a bush.

"Dang it, Leigh Ann!" Cade exclaimed, instinctively ducking his head. "Keep your britches on!"

"Listen, buster," I told him. "I've had it with you and your little secrets. So unless you fess up this very second, I can't be responsible for what I do next."

"All right, already," Cade said, caving in. "We went to Bait World, okay? It's Stink City's biggest customer and Martina wanted to check it out."

"Why would that batty old biddy want to snoop around in your family's business?" I asked.

"Because she cares deeply about catfish, Leigh Ann," he responded. "A point of view obviously lost on you."

To be honest, my neighbor was right. It was already past suppertime and the thought of a plateful of golden fried catfish fillets made my stomach growl.

"So what did you two find out?" I asked.

"Nothing much," he answered. "She just asked

the store manager how many truckloads he gets each day, what time the deliveries usually show up, and where they put it before it goes on the shelf, and then she drew a detailed map of the place—just the normal, boring questions of someone who's curious about the fish bait business, that's all."

"Doesn't sound normal to me," I scoffed.

"Not everyone is as suspicious as you are, Leigh Ann," Cade observed. "You probably think it's strange to ask about the capacity of the reservoir."

"Excuse me?" I responded. "The what?"

"The Springfield County Reservoir," he clarified. "You know—Mud Lake. Where the fishing tournament is being held next month. I'll bet you think it's strange to want to know how much water it holds."

"Who would care about an oddball fact like that?" I asked.

"Lots of people," Cade replied. "Engineers. Tourists. All the people attending the Catfish Derby."

So that's it! I thought. *They're gathering information to present at the Catfish Derby. The old biddy must be helping him with his speech!*

Well, two could play this game.

"Listen, Cade. I just had a thought," I told him. "Why don't I write the whole thing for you. That way you can concentrate on getting caught up at school."

"Write what whole thing?" Cade asked.

"Your speech, of course," I answered. "I'm sure I can come up with as many weird audience-pleasing facts as Miss What's-Her-Demon. Just leave it to me. It'll be a real corker. When you get done with these fishermen, there won't be a dry eye or a wet hook within miles. Trust me."

Cade stared with his mouth agape, like a person who can't find the right words to express his undying gratitude, or, if not that exactly, like a catfish gasping on the dock.

When I returned home, Cade's great-grandfather was leaving my house.

"Well, hello there," he greeted me. "Long time no see."

"Likewise, I'm sure," I replied politely.

From the kitchen, where dinner was cooking in a cast-iron skillet, my mother was humming a show tune, something like "I Feel Pretty."

"I just ran into Mr. Carlsen out front," I said. "Excuse me for saying this, but isn't he a little old to be your gentleman caller?"

"Sweetheart," my mother replied. "At one

hundred and seven, Mr. Carlsen is a little old even to be alive. What's your point?"

"Nothing," I said. "It just seems like you ought to be fishing in a fresher pond, that's all."

"Leigh Ann Moore!" my mother exclaimed. "I do not need your permission to choose my friends."

"Likewise, I'm sure," I responded, giving my dog a heartfelt snuggle.

Holy Jumpin' Catfish!

Here's what I thought about Miss Martina Hyde preying on my friend Cade Carlsen:

If catfish are known as bottom feeders, what are those who exploit catfish called?

Bottom-bottom feeders?

Below-bottom feeders?

Sub-bottom feeders?

Fat-bottom feeders?

I'm thinking maybe hagfish will do.

There's no nastier fish in the sea than the hagfish. With a history going back three hundred and forty million years, the disgusting habits of the eel-shaped, carrion-chomping hagfish haven't improved since day one.

With no eyes, no jaws, and no bones, the awful hagfish is nevertheless a champion at locating dead things, which it then worms its way inside of in order to devour the ghastly carcass from the inside out, all the while discharging gallons of stinking, toxic slime.

Miss Martina Hyde? I think so.

Queen Hagfish.

I'd show her!

I'd write the world's greatest treatise on the trials and tribulations of catfish. When Cade Carlsen was finished delivering it, no one would dare to harm the native underwater wildlife of the Springfield County Reservoir. It would be desecrating a sacred place.

The only problem was, I had a little trouble getting started.

Faced with a blank sheet of paper, how does one begin?

"Once upon a time . . ." I wrote, then scratched it out.

Hmm, I thought. *Writing isn't as easy as it looks.*

The next morning found me sitting motionless, sniffing the air.

A new leather chair. Mmm! A lovely aroma.

A freshly sharpened pencil. Ahh! Such a nice smell.

A bound journal, freed from the tight confines of its plastic wrapper, opened to the air for the very first time since leaving the faraway factory. China? Brazil? Downtown Kansas City?

Rich paper scent particles leapt from its pages and entertained my usually runny nose like instrumental music titillates the ears.

Scents are strongest when they're fresh, while the novelty of their molecules still fascinates our receptors. Later, sated, jaded, bored, we will ignore these smells. Be it French perfume or a Midwestern pig farm, it's all the same to a fickle nose.

The opposite of fresh is rotten.

The opposite of young is Earl Emerson Carlsen.

The opposite of me is his great-grandson, Cade.

And yet, for some strange reason that Linda Buck failed to explain, opposites do attract.

Go figure.

Sometime during the night the puppy had peed on my pillow. Upon my awakening, the room was thick, sour, and rank, and so, presumably, were those of us who'd slept in the still damp bed, but—and here's an inescapable fact of olfaction—it's hard to smell yourself, and even when you can, your brain enjoys reporting that while it can't say the same for the others, you, personally, don't stink.

Ha! I say.

When the subject comes around to odor, no one but no one can be trusted—not even yourself.

That thought gave me my first line:

"Ladies and gentlemen," I wrote, "it's not only time to wake up and smell the coffee, it's time to wake up and smell yourselves!"

Good opener, I thought. *Bound to get their attention.*

Now what I needed—what Cade needed—was the verbal equivalent of a bomb. Something so big, so impressive, so overwhelming, that these simple, God-fearing country folk would lay down their fishing poles and order up a plateful of fried chicken.

I stared at the page. Nothing else came to mind.

Did Van Gogh have this problem starting a painting? I wondered.

Had the great, troubled artist sat in his room in the sunny south of France, waiting hour after hour for an idea to come? What about Matisse? Renoir? Corot? Picasso?

Had Dickens had a hard time getting started?

Hemingway? Fitzgerald? Joyce?

How would that Proust have done it? Or the poet Emily Dickinson? Or the prairie novelist Laura Ingalls Wilder?

Famous names all.

Our brains must run on a track, because once that particular train of thought crossed the trestle, suddenly there lay before me a huge, full-blown idea.

Famous people?

Nobody is more famous than Jesus.

And guess what?

Jesus relied on fishermen for his work.

But unlike the fishermen headed for the beer-and-bratwurst Catfish Derby in Springfield, they never used a hook. In Jesus' time, so I have been told, fish were captured with nets.

And in the example provided by historical Jesus, the net was metaphorical—it was woven from words.

That's it! I realized.

Cast a net made from words over Springfield.

Fate, Coincidence, Curiosities, and Pizza

Inspired by millennia of history and religion, I carefully crafted a long, poetic, spellbinding sermon for Cade to use in Springfield, a fire-and-brimstone, give-up-your-lowdown-ways exhortation to salvation through acts of mercy, not least of which is mercy bestowed upon catfish.

Springfield is a God-fearing, Lord-loving land.

"Isn't that a catfish on the back of your wife's minivan?" I wrote. "And didn't Jesus draw this very same shape in the sand?"

"Well, then," I continued. "The rest should be obvious. What, in heaven's name, is your excuse?"

Wake up and smell the briny truth!

When I was finished with this quasi-religious mas-ter-work, even though I had improvised, fudged, and exaggerated here and there, making up stuff I knew nothing about, and interpreting for my essay's pur-pose some of the things I'd heard mentioned in church on those few occasions when I'd actually attended, I felt quite satisfied with what I'd achieved.

Job well done, Leigh Ann, I congratulated myself.

As a reward, I took a long, hot shower, during which I shampooed the dog stink from my hair, shaved my legs, and trimmed my toenails.

Some days it all just comes together, I thought.

After which, I watched TV.

In the last week of April, Chef Ludd came down with hummingbird flu, a milder but still uncomfortable form of the influenza transmitted by foreign chickens, so for several days in a row the only thing offered for lunch at Pottersville High was carry-out pizza from the Pottersville Pizza Castle.

By the third day, six hundred and forty-one students had signed a petition to retain the pizza menu permanently, dispensing with the services of Chef Ludd, but the following Monday he returned, fully recovered, and prepared gruel topped with ground pecans and raisins.

Cade simply picked at his.

"I got that speech written," I told him. "It's a real doozy, too. You're going to love it. Everybody is. I'm thinking of having it copyrighted."

"What are you talking about?" Cade asked.

"The speech you've been so worried about giving at the Catfish Derby. It's all done. I wrote it. I went over it three times looking for inconsistencies and misspelled words. I even read it out loud to Nosey. If I do say so myself, it's a humdinger. You're going to be one mighty proud kid to stand up in front of all those hayseeds, chowderheads, and throwbacks and give that speech."

"I'm not giving any speech at the Catfish Derby," Cade declared. "Why would I do that?"

"Cade Carlsen," I said with more than a little annoyance, "I distinctly remember your telling me that you were planning to make a dramatic public statement at the tournament that would fix the catfish problem once and for all."

"Oh," Cade said. "I think you may have misunderstood. When I said 'dramatic public statement,' I didn't mean a speech. I have something much more explosive in mind."

Explosive?

A raisin slid from the tines of my fork and rolled like a rabbit pellet across the cafeteria floor, where it was stepped on and squashed by Missy Rumpole, who was going back to the serving line for a second helping.

"You and that witch aren't planning to blow up the dam, are you?" I whispered in alarm. "Or shoot somebody? Or kidnap someone? Because if you are, Cade Carlsen, friend or not, I'll turn you in faster than you can say 'snitch'!"

"I really am not at liberty to discuss the details, Leigh Ann," he said. "But with so many famous fishermen gathered together at one time, it's the perfect chance to change the public's attitude for good. I mean, you'd quit eating funnel cakes if they gave you a tummy ache every time, wouldn't you?"

"To tell you the truth, Cade, they do and I have," I confessed, "but I'm still not sure what you're driving at."

"I've said too much already," Cade concluded. "If I told you any more, you'd be an accessory. I wouldn't want that to happen to you."

You know how some people are fond of remarking on coincidences? For example, they see a rainbow on their way to breakfast at Denny's and a few minutes later the girl with braces on her teeth who brings them extra sausage is wearing a nametag that says "Rainbow," so of course they feel compelled to say something (as if the poor kid's never had that happen before!).

Well, I'm not like that. I just quietly nod my head, because in my opinion everything in life is a coincidence—everything. It's all connected, and to prove it, all you have to do is take a closer look.

Here's Cade throwing me huge hints about exploding funnel cakes at the Catfish Derby, and no sooner do I walk in the door that afternoon than my mother announces she's snagged a temporary part-time job for the three days in May that we're going to be in Springfield.

"I'm in charge of pouring batter for the funnel cakes," she tells me with obvious pride. "Won't that be fun? And the funnel cake booth is right next to the Carlsens' Stink City catfish bait display, so you and Cade can visit as much as you like."

"That's great, Mom," I said. "Congratulations."

My stars! I thought. *This thing is getting curiouser and curiouser.*

Crime and Punishment

The peak season for the Stink City factory had arrived. For his own safety I kept Nosey inside, away from the wandering packs of lost dogs that were finding their way to Pottersville.

Like gossip, stink has a way of getting around.

The Carlsens took on hired hands. Dark-haired men from countries where English isn't spoken braved the frightful stench in order to send a few extra dollars home.

I could only imagine the consternation of their families when they opened the envelopes and got a whiff of American money.

Pee-yew!

This was not the America that they'd seen on *The Beverly Hillbillies*. This was a rotten America, where even the money stank to high heaven.

Cade's great-grandfather ran the bait manufacturing operation with an iron fist, keeping his distance from the factory but signing for every shipment of ingredients that FedEx, DHL, Shumpert Truck Line, UPS, and the United States Postal Service's Debra Dogwald dropped off.

As it does every year about this time, the *Pottersville Post* printed letters from the region's concerned citizens.

"It's like something out of a horror movie," a newspaper reader named Big Buster wrote. "You can't get away from it."

"Every time I go outside, I retch," Terry Moozle, a freelance mudjacker, volunteered. "Do you suppose they're burning turkey feathers over there?"

"For Jupiter's sake," Ho Chi Silverman, choir director of the First Aspirational No-Tithe Church in distant downtown Mansfield, wrote. "When the wind is right, you can't eat, you can't sleep, you can't wash your clothes, you can't even breathe."

"What you're smelling is no farm smell," an old-timer named Wallace Crossgrain summarized. "What you're smelling is the death of the town of Pottersville."

The only positive statement the paper printed came from a backwoods chicken farmer identified as Salvatore Cali. He reported, "I caught a catfish as big as a bull walrus with this rancid goop. Look for me next month in Springfield. I'll be the one holding the trophy."

Meanwhile, Miss Martina Hyde was having her hair done.

"Make me look like Garbo," she instructed the senior stylist, a chronic earwax sufferer named Tanya who was sure that Miss Hyde had said "Harpo."

In any event, fixing Miss Hyde's hair was no simple task, given the deplorable condition of the pale, dry wisps of Spanish moss that clung like strings of strained nematodes to her head. In fact, so totally devoid of life was her crown that three sittings, each a week apart, were required for Tanya to prepare Miss Hyde's hair for this occasion.

In Springfield, no occasion is more special than the annual catfish fishing tournament. What the Mardi Gras has historically been to New Orleans, the Kentucky Derby to Louisville, the Garlic Festival to Gilroy, California, and the Super Bowl to wherever it may happen to be played, the Springfield Catfish Derby is to this small but proud flat-rock town.

Preparations for the next year's tournament begin before the signs from the last one are taken down, (although, to be honest, signs often stay up for months, procrastination being a widespread trait in the Ozarks).

Even so, given the magnitude of the event, its precarious reliance not just on Mother Nature but on a far more fickle factor, the whims and international travel plans of the piscatorially famous, the final weeks before official hooks drop into the murky waters of Springfield's Mud Lake reservoir are nothing less than frantic.

Even I, more than a hundred miles away in rural Pottersville, and a person not easily seduced by fashion, was determined to obtain new clothes for the occasion.

Although we counted the pennies at our house, and clipped cents-off coupons from every issue of the *Pottersville Post*, we enjoyed the catalogs that Debra Dogwald left in our mailbox, the most compelling of which came from the leading teen fashion trendsetter, Applecrumble and Fisch.

Here was a company selling torn, worn-out jeans for sixty-five dollars, too-small cotton shirts for fifty, and plastic flip-flops that Wal-Mart offers at a dollar ninety-six for twenty dollars and up.

How can they get away with this? I asked myself.

Because they printed their name on their stuff bigger than life, that's how. I was especially impressed by the sweatpants with the word APPLE spread all the way across the butt. If I was going to be crowned Springfield's Queen Catfish—and, thanks to Cade's great-grandfather, the fix was in—I needed something that stated unequivocally to the simple folk of Springfield, "These are fancy duds."

I needed an outfit from Applecrumble and Fisch.

Which meant that I needed money, and fast.

And how does a person get money in America? There are only two ways.

Crime and personal humiliation.

WARNING: DO NOT READ THIS CHAPTER BEFORE BREAKFAST

Welcome to the Labor Force

I needed money.

The problem was, I'd never held a job. Neither did I own anything of value that I could sell, unless you count my little dog, Nosey, and, of course, I didn't.

I lived too far out in the country to work in a restaurant or a gas station or a store, even if such places could legally hire a kid my age, which technically they couldn't, unless it was a member of the immediate family who didn't want the job in the first place.

Under the circumstances, the only work that seemed possible was helping out at Cade's family's business.

I asked him about it on the way to school.

"I guess we could use somebody to help fill jars," Cade said as Gucci swerved to avoid colliding with Debra Dogwald's truck, idling in front of a row of rural mailboxes on the wrong side of the road.

"That sounds easy enough," I said. "What's it pay?"

"Minimum wage," he replied. "But you get a discount on bait and a free starter bar of soap."

"Sounds good to me," I said. "When do I start?"

"I'll have to clear it with my parents," Cade answered, "but I see no reason why you couldn't begin this afternoon."

There's a good reason that the building behind Cade's house has no windows. If strangers ever saw what was going on inside, they'd die of fright, if not asphyxiation. The place was like something out of Dante's *Inferno*, that ancient Italian poem that goes on forever about what hell is like. I never read it, of course, because I like only stories with happy endings, but I heard about it on public TV one time and it sounded perfectly dreadful. Apparently the place is filled with fire and torture and poison gas and whips and chains and people screaming and stuff while their flesh is being ripped off by devils. Ugh. It's stuff like that that gives poetry a bad name, if you ask me.

Why waste your time?

Inside the Stink City catfish bait factory, Cade's parents were hunched over a metal table with dull meat cleavers clasped in their rubber-gloved hands, chopping long-dead, tire-flattened, fur-bearing animals into bite-size bits, which, from time to time, they dumped into piles on a moving conveyor belt.

Farther down the line, Mr. Glossup, the Carlsens' versatile handyman, was stirring the steaming contents of a blood-soaked copper vat using a long-handled shovel, his face protected from deadly spatters by a welder's mask.

Other workers, new arrivals from distant lands, were busy pulling innards from rotted poultry carcasses, which they kneaded by hand into a doughlike substance by mixing in commercial liquefied rat vomit and carefully measured clumps of rancid, fuzzy blue-green cheese.

For once, words failed me. The awful smell was so horrendous that it defied my powers of description. The sounds were horrid, too: The *clunk-clunk-clunk* of blunt blades severing once-living bone. The serpent's hiss and devil's spit of boiling fat and guts. The silent screams of all the ghosts this ghastly room had ever seen.

Welcome to Stink City, I thought.

My first real job.

"Hey there, sweetheart," Cade's mother called out cheerfully from deep within the gloom. "Here's your hat. Be sure to wear it whenever you're at work."

Lani Carlsen handed me a white paper cap like the ones counter clerks in ice cream parlors wear.

"That's so your hair doesn't get into the product," Lenny Carlsen explained. "As the final filler, you're the ultimate check in Stink City's seven steps to quality control. Our customers—and the catfish they catch—are counting on you."

In my mind's eye I pictured a portly, blotchy pink man dozing in the back of a battered bass boat, a bottle of warm, flat beer in one hand and a fancy fishing rod in the other. Plastic-wrapped bologna and cheese sandwiches are floating in the tepid slop-slosh at his feet. The insistent buzz of a giant horsefly awakens him.

Yawning, he scratches his fat, sunburned stomach, sits up, and dips his fingertips into an open jar of gooey bait, at which point he is alarmed to discover that it contains a thin strand of hair from the head of a teenage girl.

"Holy cousin of Saint Christopher!" he exclaims in disgust.

Will this man ever choose this brand again?

You have to wonder.

Clearly, every job is important.

A woman named Paula Turnstile showed me to how to operate the pneumatic jar filler. My job was to squirt sludge into plastic jars, sprinkle it with a gray-white powder from an industrial-size shaker, then screw the lids on tight. Squirt, shake, twist. Squirt, shake, twist. It took some practice—every so often I'd do shake, squirt, twist, and once, unfortunately, I went twist, shake, squirt, but I finally got the hang of it. By quitting time I'd filled nearly twelve hundred twelve-ounce jars. I'd also earned fifteen dollars and forty-five cents, a third of which, for reasons that I still do not understand, the government retained to help pay for the war that nobody wanted and for social security for some rich old people in South Florida.

Also, after a few hours of working in the factory, I smelled just like a Carlsen.

"Jumpin' Jehosephat!" my mother cried when I got home, as she raced to the bathroom to barf. "Next time, Leigh Ann, wear a wetsuit!"

The Riches of the Earth

As is well accepted by now, outer space is not an empty expanse, the earth's atmosphere is not just air, its water isn't only H_2O, and the ground beneath our feet is not simply particles of dirt.

Among other things, both dead and alive, throughout the temperate regions of the world, the native soil is home to nematodes—*Caenorhabditis elegans.*

Ever since Linda Buck's presentation at Pottersville High School, when the testy one half Nobel laureate mentioned she was experimenting with nematodes to isolate the key to longevity, and Cade Carlsen shared his command of nematode trivia that he'd picked up from snooping on his great-grandfather's UPS deliveries, I felt my fundamentally superior knowledge momentarily eclipsed.

To salvage my self-esteem, I'd begun subscribing to *Professional Nematode Rancher* magazine (*PNR*), reading it from cover to cover.

Of course, as I've said before, this story is not about me. It's about Cade Carlsen, that lucky, empty-headed, odiferous little klutz. But nematodes, as it turns out, are one small but important part of the big picture.

A full-grown nematode is only about a millimeter long, so a shovelful of healthy soil can easily contain a million or more of the little critters—although you have to ask yourself, what kind of person has time to count them?

Despite their natural abundance, Cade's great-grandfather found it desirable to have his nematodes shipped from a laboratory supply company in the state of North Carolina.

"There's nematodes and there's nematodes," Mr. Carlsen said by way of explanation, an observation I could not dispute with any authority. "Anyway, why do you ask?"

"I was thinking of starting my own business," I told him. "I'm not entirely satisfied with my present job."

It stinks, I thought to myself. *It's like working inside a septic tank.*

Already, the vice principal had suggested that I ride on Cade's bus permanently.

"It's nothing personal, Leigh Ann," she had told me in that just-between-us-girls voice she sometimes affects when she's really serious about an infraction. "We just think it might get your day off to a better start with the students who bathe regularly."

"That's not a particularly large number," I replied. "In case you haven't noticed."

"We do our best, Leigh Ann," she responded. "It's no picnic for the administration, either."

"Whatever," I said, shrugging my shoulders, a mistake in the tiny office of the assistant principal since it released an unpleasant catfish bait aroma from my armpits.

"Raising a quality nematode isn't the cakewalk it may seem," Cade's great-grandfather continued. "When you're dealing with living things, there are any number of risk factors."

"I don't see how you can miss," I told him. "The little squirmers breed by the gazillions in all kinds of dirt and grow to maturity in a single day. Not only is finding them easier than fishing, which we all know any fool can do—and unfortunately does—you don't have to walk as far. I only wish I'd thought of this sooner."

"All right, Leigh Ann," Cade's great-grandfather capitulated. "It's obvious that I can't stop you from trying, so when your first crop is ready, bring them to me. If they're what I need, I'll pay you the same price I pay the laboratory."

Now we're talking, I thought, thinking of the easy money I was going to make.

Cade laughed at me when I told him of my plans.

"You'll be back at work tomorrow," he predicted.

"Oh, yeah?" I said.

Of course, the odiferous flathead turned out to have hit the nail right on its, well, how else can I put it, flat head.

The following afternoon, as Paula Turnstile hustled to keep me supplied with fresh jars, I squirted, sprinkled, and twisted on lids in the Carlsens' bait factory.

Oh, I just hate it when Cade is right!

The problem with collecting nematodes isn't finding them. Lordy, they're everywhere! It's separating them from the stuff around them. More exacting than sifting needles from haystacks, nematode harvesting is like extracting pieces of living lint from a county landfill, a task for which I have neither the patience nor the fingernails.

You go to pick one up and its fragile body disintegrates between your fingers. In no time at all, your fingertips are covered with microscopic goo and you don't have a single living nematode in your bucket.

They never mentioned this problem in *PNR*.

How was I to know?

I should write a letter to the editor.

Heck, I should cancel my subscription.

Catfish Are Different

What a dreadful job I had!

But, as I've said many times already, this narrative isn't about me—it's about my friend and neighbor, Cade Carlsen, whom I could now shadow like a red-tailed hawk following an unwary, near-blind vole.

When Cade wasn't handling great green globs of greasy grimy gopher guts on the Carlsens' hellish assembly line, he schlepped deliveries to and from the house.

His great-grandfather, he explained, didn't trust anybody else, a situation I found ironic because Cade was the only one I knew about who'd ever sold out to FISHTALE (the Foundation for the blah blah etc. Everywhere run by Miss Martina Hyde).

Families.

Who can understand them?

Like other Stink City employees, I was entitled to a break every hour. Usually Paula Turnstile, Manuel, Poco Manuel, Manuel Grande, and a gold-toothed grand-mother from Patagonia named Maria Manuel, would go outside to smoke hand-rolled cigarettes under the tallest black walnut tree in the state (one hundred and thirty-four feet before lightning took off the top twelve feet), where they all conversed happily in a rapid-fire language that I neither spoke nor understood.

Mr. Glossup typically took advantage of the time to telephone his stockbroker in the nearby town of Cabool. The Carlsens, Cade's hard-working parents, in a sacrificial effort to set a fine managerial example for the employees, remained inside and kept performing their horrid jobs on the Stink City assembly line.

Cade and I liked to stroll to the house for fresh lemonade, then sit by the pond and watch the ducks.

"This is a really crummy job," I told him. "On the other hand, most days, once we get outside, it's a very nice place to be."

"Well, there you have the essence of the dilemma," Cade said.

"What do you mean?" I asked.

"Which is more important, what you do or where you do it?" he replied.

"What you do, I guess," I answered. "Unless where you do it is even more awful."

"Exactly," he said.

Hmm, I thought.

The sweet scent of young honeysuckle perfumed the country air. On the pond, a male mallard duck, handsome in a fancy feathered suit of black and white and green, plunged his proud, iridescent head beneath the water as his dull-colored companion, a doting plump female, looked on.

"Does it ever bother you," I asked, "that you don't have many friends?"

"I have you," Cade replied. "How many friends does a person need?"

I shrugged, and though I didn't speak it out loud, the thought crossed my mind that there's no such thing as too many friends.

Or so I've been led to believe.

But how many friends can you really be a friend to? Realistically, there must be a point at which you are physically and emotionally incapable of responding to everybody.

"You know most species of fish congregate in schools," Cade continued, "by the scores, the hundreds, even the thousands. In fact, in the ocean, cruise ships have reported sightings of schools of fish that from end to end extend for more than fifty miles.

"Catfish are different," he pointed out. "For the most part, they're solitary creatures, preferring to lie low during the day and venture out only at sunup and sundown. Catfish are more like hermits. They enjoy their privacy."

"Interesting," I said. "I never knew that."

My sense of intellectual superiority was wilting before Cade's onslaught of detailed information, like a handful of wild violets left on the porch railing.

Could I have misjudged Cade?

Could he be smarter than I thought?

Could he, heaven forbid, actually be smart?

There was much more that Cade would teach me during our breaks from the assembly line. Some of it was of a practical nature, if you consider learning the ins and outs of the stinkbait business to be practical.

For example, there are a number of ways to catch a catfish, he explained, and among the most effective are the use of fresh bait, such as shrimp, night-crawlers, or chicken livers; fresh cutbait, such as dissected parts of carp, herring, suckers, and shad; and the wonderful world of dipbaits and doughbaits, also known as stinkbaits.

This last category is sometimes combined with one of the first two—that is, some fishermen like to coat a baby shad with dipbait, for example; more often, they'll use a plastic dipworm or sponge with a treble hook attached.

The decision depends on where you're fishing: whether you're in the middle of a river with a strong current, or floating silently in a quiet reservoir within spitting distance of the bank.

Back when Cade's great-grandfather started the company, there were only three commercial stinkbait manufacturers in the country.

Today there are dozens, including mom-and-pop enterprises operating out of garages. Unlike the venerable Stink City brand, the smaller companies tend to come and go, with one going quite dramatically a few years back when barrels of decomposing secret ingredients produced enough flammable methane that when the proprietor paused to puff on a cigar, his garage door blew out and landed in the street where some kids happened to be skateboarding.

Fortunately, no one was seriously injured,

although the lawsuits went back and forth for years.

The point is, nothing is as simple as it may seem, and where catfish are involved, it's even more of a problem.

Cheaters Often Win

Shadowing Cade at work was proving to be an education, and I'm not just talking about how to fill a jar with goop.

Among other things, I was beginning to understand how scientific advancements consistently outpace our capacity for compassion.

"Did you know," Cade observed, "that many fishermen now use satellite global positioning systems, sonar, and underwater cameras to locate their quarry?"

"Where's the challenge in that?" I replied.

"It's not about challenge," Cade explained. "It's about winning."

"Hmm," I said.

"When I was a little kid," Cade continued, idly tossing a pebble into the pond and watching the circles spread from one bank to the other, "I stepped on ants, not accidentally, but on purpose.

"Once, I dropped lit matches down the anthill's entrance," he confessed. "Another time I took a hose to flood the inhabitants out.

"When I was ten years old, my parents gave me a twenty-two-caliber rifle for Christmas. Right away, I went out to see what I could find. Not far from where we're sitting, I spied a brown lizard swaying atop a blade of grass, warming itself in the weak winter sun.

"I froze, planted my legs apart, sighted carefully, and squeezed the trigger," he said. "Instantly the lizard blew apart into bits of flesh and skin and blood and organs, leaving nothing behind that looked remotely like a lizard.

"I couldn't believe the destruction—how sudden, how easy, how complete it was," he said, with obvious remorse. "A single shot. The first time I ever fired a gun. It was also the last time.

"I know there are lots of people who disagree with what I'm telling you, Leigh Ann," Cade said, "but as far as I'm concerned, killing anything for sport is wrong."

"Lizards feel pain," I responded, expressing my understanding.

"That lizard felt nothing of the kind," Cade

corrected me. "For him, it was over instantly. The only pain that day was felt by me."

For some reason, I patted Cade's hand.

When the occasion is worth remembering, humankind builds a memorial. India's opulent Taj Mahal was created to celebrate a wedding. The great pyramids of Egypt mark the deaths of Pharaohs. On a more modest note, international exhibitions have spurred people to erect such achievements as the Eiffel Tower in Paris, the Space Needle in Seattle, and the World's Largest Concrete Prairie Dog in Dudley, Kansas.

Although you might not guess it from their dental work, the people of Springfield are just like the people in the rest of the world. Among the evidence for this claim is that for the Greater Springfield Invitational Catfish Derby the city fathers agreed that it was high time to improve the appearance of the boat ramp that descended like a load of spilled tar from the highway into the Springfield County Reservoir.

To this end, a citywide contest was decreed. Each of Springfield's leading architectural firms was invited to submit designs.

With twenty-seven such professional firms listed in

the Greater Springfield Yellow Pages, organizers were certain that the city would ultimately enjoy a structure over the boat ramp that would be every bit as sensational as the soaring gateway to the West, the famous St. Louis Arch.

Unfortunately, Springfield's architects have little time to devote to speculative competitive work, being bogged down with such high-paying gigs as church parking lots, twenty-four-hour self-storage centers, and objets d'art for souvenir stands on the road to Branson.

Only one firm took the time to reply to the city's request for a proposal. Fortunately, or so the city fathers thought at the time, this was the prestigious partnership of Van Cleef & Arpels, believed by many to be the best in the Ozarks.

But what the city fathers didn't know was that the proposal that arrived on the luxurious Van Cleef & Arpels letterhead had been created not by a licensed architect and member of the firm, but by an unqualified, middle-aged, amoral harridan hired to clean the company's offices when the regular cleaning woman, Isabella Francesca, was indisposed by food poisoning contracted at the Pottersville Country Corner Cafe.

"It was the sun-dried chicken gizzards that did it,"

Isabella Francesca gasped in a call to her employer's antique answering machine, to which she added garbled instructions to sue the plasterers, a suggestion that, to the office manager who transcribed the message, made no sense at all.

As fate would have it, this shameful architectural subterfuge was perpetrated on Springfield's gullible civic leadership by none other than the bane of my existence, the dreadful, cold-hearted, and malevolent Miss Martina Hyde.

"The fools!" she shouted, hooting like a great horned owl. "Now I've got them!"

The Devil Is in the Details

Miss Martina Hyde was a woman who, in another place and time, would have sent Snow White to perish in the forest at the hands of a dolt of a woodsman. That she was now loose in Springfield, driving a BMW convertible and having her way with the volunteer management of the Springfield Catfish Derby, speaks volumes about the insights into the human psyche possessed by the earlier management at Disney.

This woman was not just a witch. She was evil to the core.

"Hee, hee, hee," she laughed in that characteristic way that cartoon witches do.

Clearly, she had put a great deal of thought into her boat ramp design. With two goals in mind, the first being winning the contest and the second being creating as much havoc as her demented mind could conceive, she came up with an idea that was truly original.

Her uncontested entry consisted of twin cast-iron reproductions of the biggest catfish ever caught in the world—two matching likenesses.

Each was more than eleven feet long.

According to the specifications of her prizewinning design, the fish sculptures were to be suspended from enormous fishhooks on forty-foot titanium fishing rods installed on opposite sides of the present boat ramp.

Her idea was that the titanium rods, tugged by the weight of the cast-iron sculptures, would bend gently toward each other, suspending the fish art high in the air, where they would dangle like a giant mobile over a baby's crib, swaying in the gentle breezes from the glistening state reservoir and forming a tall, ever-changing, and graceful archway over the public access to Mud Lake, or, as Miss Hyde described it in her proposal to the committee, "creating a piscatorial, curved Calderesque bower that beckons from afar, 'Howdy, y'all, come on down.'"

The ramp itself she proposed to surface with rolled linoleum, gaily printed with interlocking triangular shapes of various colors, "an homage to our city's trailer park heritage," she explained.

With nothing else to choose from, and due largely to the implied credentials afforded by the stolen Van Cleef & Arpels stationery signed by the entrant "M. Hyde, Esq., Member, Architectural Association of Northern Rhodesia," the city fathers shrugged their collective shoulders and rubber-stamped the proposal, after which they sent Miss Hyde a check for ten thousand dollars, directed to her home address, as she had insisted, for the exclusive rights to build her innovative monument to catfishing that, she assured them in closing, would unequivocally put the city of Springfield on the map.

Had Miss Hyde studied architecture in college instead of demonology, it's possible that she could have made something of herself. In its suitability for the setting, her "dangling twin giant catfish" concept revealed a modest degree of natural talent.

Where it ultimately fell short was where so many seemingly great ideas fall short—in the details. For although Miss Hyde's brainstorm was based on recreating and duplicating the biggest catfish on record—six hundred and forty-six pounds dripping wet, a record set in Thailand in 2005—she'd failed to consider that the specific gravity of cast iron is substantially greater than that of catfish flesh.

When the twin sculptures were cast at the Ozark Yard Art Foundry under the supervision of Mrs. Charles (Tammi) Bennett, foreman, they each weighed as much as a Toyota Tercel.

A lesser class of leadership might have thrown up its hands and never recovered from such a setback, but the city fathers of Springfield, feeling the Catfish Derby deadline breathing down their stubby and, in many cases, hairy necks, debated their dilemma for less than sixty seconds.

"Hang the dang things," Chairman Fritz declared, and with that the deed was done.

Unfortunately, when installed at the site, Miss Hyde's artistic vision was severely compromised, for not only did her catfish not dangle, they bent their supporting rods nearly double, causing the sculptures to remain motionless, like fat, oblong Henry Moore anchors on the ground.

"If you stand over to one side," Chairman Fritz pointed out optimistically, "it looks sort of like two arches."

Meanwhile, with ten days to go until the Catfish Derby, the shores of Mud Lake were being transformed.

Tents, booths, kiosks, stands, card tables, and gazebos were going up as fast as the hillbilly workers could assemble them, which, to be truthful about it, is not very fast.

Perhaps the most ambitious of these exhibits was the Stink City Grand Pavilion.

Inspired by the legendary Crystal Palace created for the World's Fair in London in 1851, but on a much smaller scale, the Grand Pavilion was made entirely from dis-carded window glass, much of it scavenged from area front yards and ditches, the result being a glistening jewel box of sorts for the presentation of the Carlsens' most famous—and only—product.

The scene was set for Springfield's biggest unnatural disaster.

Countdown to Derby Day

Having earned enough money for a new outfit, I quit my factory job for good, placed my order with Applecrumble and Fisch, and skipped school to give myself time to shower off the stink.

That same day, the *Pottersville Post* reported that a truckload of Stink City catfish bait bound for the giant retailer Bait World had failed to arrive. Authorities speculated that the driver probably decided to return home to Honduras, adding that as soon as they're not so busy getting ready for the Catfish Derby, they'll conduct an investigation.

In the back of my mind, I had a vague feeling that Cade and Miss Martina Hyde had something to do with the missing shipment, but I was too excited about finally being free from Carlsenstink after so many weeks to give it further thought.

The fact was, I had literally come to my senses. I could smell again. So, while momentarily intrigued by the news item, I found myself far more attracted to the crisp, clean, invigorating scent of the newsprint itself.

Reading the newspaper is interesting, I concluded,

but sniffing it is a rich, fulfilling experience.

I ran into the kitchen and began pulling spices off the rack, slowly inhaling each one: Nutmeg. Cinnamon. Sweet basil. Oregano. Sage.

Ah! I thought. *This is the life!*

Alas, there's a price to be paid by the sentry who leaves her post, however briefly. That afternoon, on the one day I took a break from shadowing Cade, he disembarked from his semiprivate school bus with Missy Rumpole, that perpetual nuisance, her nose casting a shadow on the ground like Puxatawney Phil standing fully upright in the February sun.

Oh, no! I thought in a panic. *Surely this isn't jealousy I'm feeling!*

That night, I moped around the house while my mother studied the materials Debra Dogwald had delivered from McFunnel's.

"I've never seen so many pages in an employment contract," my mother said, exasperated. "All I'm doing is pouring batter for a couple of days, but from the way this thing reads, you'd think I was being hired to keep the Mud Lake dam from being blown up by terrorists."

"McFunnel's is a big company, Mom," I pointed

out. "They're probably worried that somebody will try to steal their secret recipe."

"I suppose," she agreed, "but it seems awfully silly to me. Did Mr. Carlsen ask you to sign anything before you went to work in his factory?"

"Nope," I replied. "He just suggested that I wear a clothespin on my nose."

"Good advice," my mother muttered, dutifully scribbling her initials on the bottom of each page.

If a person cheats at cards, or golf, or baseball, or any of a number of other sports, there can be dire consequences, including fines and public humiliation. But when the sport is fishing, the rules are as bendable as Gumby.

Fishermen are *expected* to cut corners, to work the angles, to out-and-out lie. In fact, if you look it up in a thesaurus, one of the synonyms for *falsehood* is *fish story*.

So it should come as no surprise that the professional crowd now descending on Springfield was made up largely of swindlers, brigands, con artists, flimflammers, and modern-day pirates.

The official regulations of the tournament acknowledged this unsavory characteristic among its clientele:

Top finishers are required to pass a polygraph test.
Additional tests, including random examinations
of the catch, may be given at the discretion of
tournament officials. Nets, spears, guns, explo-
sives, poisons, or cormorants are not allowed. Any
artificially preserved, packaged, frozen, breaded,
or filleted catfish will be disqualified. All entries
are subject to inspection by a state-licensed fish
veterinarian. All fish must be able to flop when
prodded.

Within a crowd such as this, despite her singular manner and appearance, Miss Martina Hyde could do little to call attention to herself.

Indeed, as the FISHTALE founder skulked about the Catfish Derby grounds, setting up her surprise with, I suspected, the assistance of her naive young ward, Cade Carlsen, and his newly acquired dimwit sidekick, the nasally superior Missy Rumpole, Miss Hyde seemed no more peculiar than a fat-butted clown at the circus.

But, of course, as we all know, even if all they're asking you to do is smell a flower, clowns are not to be trusted.

The Astonishing Lure of Catfish

My clothes arrived from Applecrumble and Fisch and they fit me like a glove. Literally. It looked as if I were wearing a catcher's mitt.

The pants were nothing like the picture in the catalog. Even the name on the seat was different. Instead of APPLE, a word with appealing connotations, the big white letters emblazoned across my rear end spelled out FISCH.

"How can they get away with this?" I complained to my mother, looking as if I were suiting up for a sack race at church camp.

"Well," she observed, "they do seem a little unstructured, and not especially flattering, but sometimes you have to make sacrifices for fashion."

"I look ridiculous," I said. "And it's too late to send them back."

"Oh, they're not that bad," she said unconvincingly.

Here's a fact worth remembering: If something is for sale, it's because the person who owns it doesn't want it.

Others in the neighborhood were also getting new

clothes. The 107-year-old Earl Emerson Carlsen, realizing he'd outlived his tuxedo by decades, was being fitted for a rental by Pottersville's leading—and only—tailor, the Japanese-born Kenneth "Mr. Ken" Yomato.

"Pink is very popular these days," Mr. Ken advised. "Also wide lapels in powder blue."

"I'm told that raw fish is popular in your homeland," the senior Carlsen countered. "That doesn't mean I'll ever eat it."

"Black it is," Mr. Ken replied, dropping to one knee to measure the elderly bait magnate's inseam, which proved to be not a straight line, but a parabolic curve that ran from his hipbones to his feet.

Hmm, thought Mr. Ken. *Perhaps this was the real inspiration for the St. Louis Arch.*

In fact, all the Carlsens were getting costumed for their roles in the upcoming event. Working the Stink City exhibit during the Springfield Catfish Derby was an important family tradition.

"This is where we put a face on the smell," Cade's father explained. "Our customers know our product, but for them to truly love our product, they need to know us, too."

"It's roadkill, rancid blood, and putrefied offal,

and it stinks to high heaven," Cade pointed out. "What's to love?"

"Now, Cade," his mother admonished, "let's not be difficult."

Excitement surrounding the Catfish Derby had also afflicted the pages of the *Pottersville Post*. The paper was usually Pottersville's most comprehensive source for local goings-on, but in recent days it seemed that every article bore the dateline of Springfield.

The story eliciting the greatest number of letters to the editor was an examination of the rivalries among three towns: Savannah, Tennessee; Belzoni, Mississippi; and Des Allemands, Louisiana. Each claimed to be paramount in the increasingly competitive world of catfish, contentions that boosters in Springfield now rose to dispute.

Billing itself as "Catfish Capital of the World," a phrase it eventually trademarked, the city of Savannah traces its first catfish derby back to 1952. Had a mercury spill not poisoned the river in 1962, resulting in a thirty-one-year time-out, Savannah might find it easier to fend off challengers today.

But the business of rural tourism abhors a vacuum, no matter how unfortunate its cause, so into the breach stepped little Belzoni, which, in the mid-1970s, persuaded the governor of Mississippi to award it the designation of "Catfish Capital of the World."

The only problem with Belzoni's opportunistic grab for fame is that its catfish all live side by side on catfish farms, vast man-made ponds where the catfish are jammed together like caged chickens at Tyson.

"You could walk on the backs of Belzoni catfish for fifteen miles and never get your feet wet," a Springfield spokesman said.

Then there's the Louisiana bayou town of Des Allemands. Like Belzoni, in the mid-1970s Des Allemands civic leaders convinced their governor to award them the title "Catfish Capital of the World." When this failed to produce the desired results, they then persuaded the state legislature to try "Catfish Capital of the Universe," a prize they received from the Louisiana lawmakers in 1980.

"They're dreaming," an anonymous Springfielder wrote, "but at least their catfish are wild."

The festival in Springfield, while not the nation's biggest when measured by annual attendance, is said to be the most passionate celebration of its kind, a fact that city fathers admit may be hard to prove.

"But you can feel it, you can taste it, and you can smell it whenever you wet your hook in Springfield," the *Pottersville Post* quoted the deputy mayor Hugo Bassett as saying.

As for me, I didn't care whether this was the biggest deal of its kind or just another deal. I was simply happy to be getting out of Pottersville.

The Road to Stardom

For my mother and me, the drive down Highway 60 marked the start of a grand adventure. After my father died, money was tight in our house, so travel of any sort, even to someplace as close by as Springfield, was a luxury.

We decided to bring Nosey with us, inasmuch as he was now a part of our family. During Derby Week, we figured, the motel people would have much bigger fish to fry than somebody's sweet little puppy.

By "sweet" I am referring to Nosey's disposition, not to the odors he was giving off inside our closed car. I'd made the mistake of feeding him dinner scraps the night before, which had upset his delicate, immature digestive system.

"My stars, Leigh Ann," my mother said, slowing to a near stop to let an Amish man in a horse-drawn buggy pull onto the road. "If he does this in our motel room, they'll make us leave for sure."

At the Country Mart in Seymour, we bought a can of aerosol spray in a fragrance called "Russian Linen." After a quick and successful fumigation, Nosey curled into a ball and went to sleep, and I practiced waving my hand from the car window like a queen.

Queen Catfish.

Not a very pretty-sounding title, but I was thinking it might turn out to be one of those things I could tell my children about.

Cade, I remembered, didn't want children. All he wanted was to feel sorry for himself by feeling sorry for catfish, and possibly to blow up the dam as well, which, when you think about it, is not likely to be very helpful to the catfish currently enjoying their docile, bottom-dwelling lives in Mud Lake.

Well, a person like that *shouldn't* have children.

Queen Catfish. It does have a certain ring to it.

Of course, my debut into royalty was just a cover. My real assignment was to save Cade Carlsen from himself, not to mention from the clutches of Miss Martina Hyde and Missy Rumpole.

You'd think that a girl with a honker like Missy Rumpole's would steer clear of a boy who smells like an open sewer, there being so much more nasal area to capture the noxious odor.

Possibly it was pheromones. And possibly she was doing it just to give me a hard time.

Cade was already in Springfield.

He'd left the night before, riding with the direction-challenged Gucci at the helm of the bus, accompanied by his great-grandfather, his parents, two of their employees—Paula Turnstile and Mr. Glossup—Missy Rumpole's uncle, and Missy Rumpole, whose nose presumably required a seat all its own.

From time to time, I looked along the roadside to see if they might have crashed, but all I saw were paper cups, plastic Wal-Mart bags, dead armadillos, and the occasional athletic shoe.

Just east of Springfield, my mother and I found ourselves stuck in a long line at a roadblock.

Law enforcement officials, tipped off by an anonymous caller that terrorist activities were planned for the derby, were taking no chances.

Of course, the anonymous caller was myself.

Who else was going to do the right thing?

"Are you carrying any weapons, explosives, or sharp metal objects in the vehicle?" a highway patrolman demanded of two men in a pickup truck in front of us.

"Just our pistols, hunting rifles, and shotguns," they admitted. "Plus skinning knives, fishhooks, frog gigs, lances, and lures. Oh, and five-gallon jugs of gasoline, a gross of road flares, and a case of Tennessee whiskey. Only the stuff we need for the fishing tournament."

"Okay, then," the patrolman replied, motioning for the truck to move on. "But be sure to buckle up."

"If I had a seat belt that would fit my waistline, I would," the driver said.

The patrolman got a good chuckle out of that one.

When it was our turn, the same cop confiscated my mother's fingernail file.

"It's all right," she concluded when we were back on the road. "It's a small enough sacrifice to help keep our country safe."

At the Fisherman's Inn, we were escorted to the Angler's Suite, where, to our surprise, a fruit basket was waiting on top of the minibar.

"There's a note," I said.

"Read it," my mother directed.

"'Welcome to Springfield and best wishes for a show-stopping performance,'" I read aloud. "It's signed, 'The Greater Springfield Invitational Catfish Derby Organizing Committee.'"

"Well, isn't that nice," my mother said.

"What performance?" I asked. "What show?"

Nosey, excited by his new surroundings, yawned, stretched his back legs, and proceeded to produce a stain on the carpet as big as a Frisbee.

"Maybe he should sleep in the bathtub," my mother suggested.

Carnivale!

I ran into Cade at the Fisherman Inn's complimentary breakfast buffet.

"Where's your new best friend?" I asked, as I helped myself to a stack of thin, leathery pancakes and slipped some warmed-over sausages into a paper napkin for my dog.

"Oh," Cade replied with a start, "I don't know what you mean."

"You know exactly what I mean, Cade Carlsen," I said.

"Lighten up, Leigh Ann," he pleaded. "This is not easy for me. I've got a lot on my mind."

Fuming, I said nothing in reply, calming myself by counting backwards from one hundred and breathing in the aroma of baked blueberry muffins.

"If what you're mad about is Missy Rumpole being here, that was my great-grandfather's idea," Cade explained. "He said it would be good for business."

"Excuse me?" I said.

"The publicity," Cade clarified. "With Missy Rumpole's uncle's newspaper connections, the Stink City exhibit is sure to get media coverage."

"I see," I said. "So when you're not fetching things for that lunatic fish-woman with the flashy clothes, you're seducing super-schnozes from the high school to expand your great-grandfather's fortune? What does this say about you, Cade Carlsen? Is there anybody with a sense of decency living inside your feeble head?"

I didn't wait for an answer. I set my plate on the table and stormed out of the restaurant. Later, in my motel room, because I knew Nosey would understand, I gobbled down a couple of his sausages before giving him the rest.

While my mother dressed for her debut at McFunnel's, I put on my new pants from Applecrumble and Fisch, a cotton T-shirt, and Keds, brushed my hair back and tied it into a ponytail, and tried to think of something clever to say when they crowned me queen.

Unfortunately, what kept overtaking my thoughts was the speech I'd written for Cade.

Ladies and gentlemen, I heard myself thinking, *wake up and smell the catfish! Ask yourselves, what would Jesus do? Isn't it likely that he'd prefer trout, or scallops, or maybe a nice piece of white bass with curried couscous?*

My mother and I were not prepared for the sight that greeted us at the Catfish Derby grounds. All around us surged a reservoir of humanity, a seething, shoulder-to-shoulder, amusement-starved crowd such as you might expect at a rock concert, or waiting for a ride down Magic Mountain.

There were balloon artists, face painters, banjo players, and mimes; contortionists, Irish dancers, and poets reading rhymes; pickpockets, Shriners, and all-boy choirs; Civil War reenactors, priests, monks, and friars; cowboys, lumberjacks, Geisha girls, and cops; families with fathers putting kids on top of ponies while mothers, walking backwards, kept taking snapshots.

Down one side of the lake stretched an arcade, where a dollar bill and a lot of luck would win you a basketball, a key chain, a stuffed snake, or a set of painted plates.

On the other side were fortunetellers, politicians, corn dog carts, and kiosks selling T-shirts with scenes of fishermen landing catfish as big as alligators.

"Holy macaroni!" I exclaimed. "Would you look at this place!"

"I'll catch up with you later, Leigh Ann," my mother said. "Right now I'd better get to work. I don't want to be late on my very first day."

According to the letter Debra Dogwald had delivered to our house, I was due to appear at the judge's stand at ten a.m.

I glanced at the clock at the Italian gelato stand. I had almost an hour to kill.

Meeting the judges was simply a courtesy, I assumed, since Cade's great-grandfather had engineered a slam-dunk first-place finish on my behalf.

Is this cheating? I asked myself.

Not really, I answered myself. *It's more like planning ahead.*

Anyway, it's a fishing contest, I thought, *for criminy's sake. What do people expect is going to happen?*

I hoped that the crown would be pretty.

I wondered, *Do they use real jewels?*

I figured the deal would go something like this: I'd introduce myself, accept my award, make a brief, polite thank-you speech, being sure to name each of the judges, then hightail it out of Dodge so I could get back to shadowing Cade, whose recent behavior strongly suggested that he'd benefit from supervision.

Once I was sure my crown fit properly, I'd run over to the dam and talk him out of whatever mischief he and his evil advisors had up their sleeves.

I didn't plan to take a policeman along because, honestly, I didn't want the little twerp to get into trouble he couldn't get out of.

The fact was, I liked Cade Carlsen.

Maybe it was pheromones.

Maybe it was pity.

Maybe it was simply proximity.

Queen Catfish

The time was at hand.

Within the hour, I presumed, I would be crowned Queen Catfish, an honor that, by now, I had no doubt was well deserved.

Working my way through the swarms of hill-williams, I bought a turkey leg, a frozen custard, Pop Rocks, and a spicy catfish taco, which I washed down with a cherry lemonade.

It was a hot day in Springfield, a midmorning in mid-May that felt like midsummer, thanks to our president's firm commitment to global warming.

I won fifty-five tickets playing skee-ball that I exchanged for a fortunetelling fish, which, if you've never been fortunate enough to own one, is a fish-shaped strip of cellophane that can predict the future simply by curling in the heat of your hand.

Will I ever have a boyfriend? I asked it.

Not likely, it replied.

Alone, I rode the Flaming Fishhook, a low-to-the-ground roller coaster that on its final descent passes through a circle of flickering neon meant to simulate a ring of fire.

Upon disembarking, even the little kids pleaded,

"Next time, please, let's do something else."

I was late getting to the judges' stand. It was hardly my fault. The crowds, as I've mentioned, were as thick as thieves, probably because they were thieves, not to mention an appallingly sweaty bunch.

An underarm deodorant stand would make a nice addition here, I thought.

Upon arriving at the designated spot, I was horrified to witness a costumed four-year-old girl singing "The Wind Beneath My Wings." Flapping in the breeze over her curly red ringlets was a banner reading, WELCOME, MISS JUNIOR CATFISH.

Miss Junior Catfish? I thought. *What gives?*

A few questions and a minor tantrum later, I had learned that what gave was this:

I'd been hoodwinked by that dissembling old geezer back in Pottersville.

Cade's great-grandfather hadn't even tried to sign me up for Queen Catfish. He'd stuck me in the kids' division, with contestants aged three to twelve, where the top prize was no better than what Bubba was winning on the Mud Lake midway by throwing softballs at milk bottles.

Dang! I thought. *I came all the way to Springfield for a shot at a stuffed monkey?*

Man, was I mad!

It gets worse.

When they announced the next contestant, guess who it turned out to be?

None other than Missy Rumpole and her nose!

If ever a person was persuaded to give up, it was me. Had it not been for the fact that I was wearing embarrassing contemporary fashion, I might have succumbed. But a will to live long enough to redeem my image stayed my hand.

I know, I know, I've said this story is not about me, it's about my neighbor, Cade Carlsen. But please, you have to appreciate the turmoil I was going through.

This was a world-class catastrophe!

In the same annoying voice in which she'd interrogated partial Nobel Prize winner Linda Buck at Pottersville High, Missy Rumpole recited a poem, which may have been "Charge of the Light Brigade," although I'm not sure because at that point I had my fingers in my ears.

Here's something I'll bet your mother never taught you: After things go from bad to worse, they go from worse to unbearable. While Missy Rumpole was taking her bow, the judges called my name.

What could I do?

I had nothing. No tap dance, no instrument, no repertoire of jokes, no baton, and certainly no song in my heart.

But fortune favors the prepared mind.

I gave them the sermon I'd written for Cade.

"Wake up and smell the coffee!" I exhorted the crowd of strangers. "Wake up and smell the catfish!"

Now, it isn't that people the world over aren't serious about religion, but in the area in which Springfield is but a tiny part live some especially God-fearing folks. They show up for church every Sunday without complaint, and not infrequently attend religious events on Wednesday nights. They pick up neighbors who need a ride and cook meals for members who suffer a personal loss.

In short, these are the people who don't wait for the government to get involved—they step right up and take care of one another.

They are modern-day Good Samaritans.

These well-meaning people are the backbone of our country, in many ways, much like our nation's foundersexcept for the slaves, the mansions, the powdered wigs, and the general disdain for women. So when I suggested that Jesus, as mankind's

137

shepherd, might have felt compassion for creatures as lowly as the slimy, bottom-feeding catfish, they didn't boo me off the stage.

Instead, they listened politely.

When I was through, no one clapped, but the silence that greeted me was more profound than any applause. It was as if I'd planted an idea that only needed watering; after which, given time and sunlight, it might grow.

But perhaps I'm overstating the sophistication of attendees at the Springfield Catfish Derby. It's possible that they were simply waiting for the next act.

Nothing but Trouble

"Thank you for that thoughtful presentation, Leigh Ann," the master of ceremonies said, looking not at me but at the audience. "And now, our next contestant will play three popular selections on her accordion."

Of course, I didn't win.

But neither, thank goodness, did Missy Rumpole. The honor, so called, went to a kid from Sedalia whose talent was memorizing biographies of U.S. presidents.

There would be no crown for me that day. Not Queen Catfish. Not even Miss Junior Catfish.

Seeking sympathy, I shoved through the crowd to McFunnel's to see my mother, but after waiting in line for half an hour, I learned she'd stepped out.

"I'll tell her you were here, honey," promised a smiling, sweaty woman in batter-spattered glasses.

Remembering my mission, I hoofed it down to the dam, a wide earthen barricade topped by a two-lane road connecting East Springfield to West Springfield. Below lay houses, schools, shopping centers, parks, and the imposing seven-story headquarters of the Fried Catfish Restaurant Owners Association of North America, with its sprawling training facility, Hush Puppy University.

If somebody really wanted to, I realized, *they could do a lot of harm here.*

At that moment, a red BMW rounded the bend, and, its driver having seen me by the side of the road, made a screeching U-turn and sped back the way it had come. The sticker on its back bumper was as plain as the nose on you-know-who's face: Fish Feel Pain®.

Something very fishy is going on, I thought.

I returned to McFunnel's, where my mother was pouring batter from a plastic pitcher onto steaming griddles all in a row. The restaurant was filled with clouds of vanilla and powdered sugar, an aroma that's a lot like Christmas.

"I'm not Queen Catfish," I told her.

"That's all right," my mother replied. "Have a funnel cake. It's better than being queen."

I'll have to admit, it was plenty tasty.

I found Cade at the Stink City greenhouse next door, stacking jars of packaged catfish bait into pyramids. There was no sign of Missy Rumpole. In fact, there was no sign of anyone else at all. Unlike the teeming midway outside, the only visitor in the elaborate Stink City exhibit was me.

"Smells pretty bad in here," I observed.

"It's all this sunlight on the jars," Cade explained, his voice betraying his dismay. "It heats them up so much, they give off fumes."

"Hmm," I said. "Seems like somebody should have thought of that."

Cade looked terrible. His face was flushed. His breathing was short. Sweat dripped from the tip of his nose. His eyes, normally among his more attractive features, conveyed a strange and haunted look, darting back and forth from me to the door like little cockroaches trapped in a jar.

It occurred to me that the nauseating gases forming inside this place might be poisonous.

"Are you okay, Cade?" I asked him.

"I think I made a big mistake," he confessed. "We may all be in grave danger."

"Then let's get out of here," I replied. "Just lock up. Nobody's coming here. They're all going to the weigh-in."

More people than I ever imagined, in fact.

Like fat olives stuffed into a jar, or silvery snack fish laid nose to tail in a flat-bottomed can, the onlookers, rubberneckers, gawkers, contestants, curiosity-seekers, and out-of-towners were packed together all around the judges' stand.

Off to the side, people parted to let a parade of noisy pickups try to pull their boats out of Mud Lake. Contributing to the chaos was Miss Hyde's numbskull design. Her specifications called for a slick linoleum surface on the naturally steep incline, assuring that trucks would find no traction.

One by one, they struggled to haul their heavy loads from the water, spinning chrome-covered wheels until their tires smoked, slipping and sliding from side to side, bashing their costly watercraft against the cast-iron fish sculptures like waves pounding on rocks.

By the end of the first day of the Greater Springfield Invitational Catfish Derby, half the itinerant fishing fleet had been lost to a fundamental architectural flaw. In terms of the number of boats destroyed, what Miss Martina Hyde had accomplished, through a unique combination of determined malfeasance and incurable ineptitude, was worse than the attack on the United States Navy at Pearl Harbor, Hawaii, in 1941.

And then it began to rain.

Don't Drink the Water

The middle of May is the rainy season, the time when thunderstorms tumble down the Rockies and roll across the plains, watering crops, filling rivers, and spinning out tornadoes with the power to obliterate everything in their paths.

At this time of year, rain—even a light rain—is something to pay attention to. Today's steady drizzle could become next week's raging flood. Ah, but when lightning crackles across the sky and sounds its fearsome thunder, the air, electrified, smells wonderful!

Amid mounting boat wrecks and the oncoming storm, the judges weighed the arriving catfish.

"Entry five-zero-five: nineteen pounds, seven ounces," came the announcement over the public-address system, words that were followed by applause, a handful of jeers, a brain-painful screech of electronic feedback, and a sustained buzz indicating a lightning strike in the vicinity.

"I'm not joking, Leigh Ann," Cade said. "There's big trouble."

The wind picked up and the rain began assaulting us sideways.

"Entry five-zero-five is disqualified," the loudspeaker continued. "Lead weights in the fish's gut."

The crowd responded to the news with an outburst of whistles, boos, cursing, and laughter.

"Everyone at the tournament is in peril," Cade added.

"Entry seven-six-two," the loudspeaker announced. "Twenty-two pounds, two ounces."

Again came clapping and catcalls.

"It's the reservoir," Cade went on.

"Disqualified," the announcer called as the electronic amplification of his voice rose and fell. "Entry is bearing a printed product code."

Hissing rose from the throng.

"Cade," I told him, misunderstanding the source of his anxiety, "you need to quit hanging around crazy people and start thinking for yourself."

"Entry one-one-nine," the judge announced, "weighing sixty-four pounds, is disqualified because it's the wrong kind of animal. Ladies and gentlemen, I remind you that this is a single-species contest."

"Did anybody actually catch a catfish today?" my mother asked.

As the thinning crowd of spectators became soaked to the bone, only two catfish passed muster for posting on the leader board, a three-pound channel cat turned in by a professional team called the Fat Bottom Feeders, and the other, weighing a modest two pounds, nine ounces, landed by Missy Rumpole's uncle.

It was dinnertime before conversation among the key players in this drama could resume.

Because we'd identified ourselves as paying with vouchers, a medium of exchange on which the Crazy Cajun Catfish Cafe made no money, we found ourselves seated between the swinging doors to the kitchen and the restrooms.

As in many themed restaurants, the signs identifying the restrooms were of a creative nature, with a male catfish signifying the men's room and a female catfish marking the door to the women's room. The trouble with this is that unless you're a catfish or an ichthyologist with a scalpel, there's no way to distinguish one gender from the other. Consequently, throughout our meal we were interrupted by voices saying, "Excuse me" and "Oh, I'm so sorry" and "What in the world do you think you're doing?"

Add to this the exchanges typical of a busy commercial kitchen, in which a high-strung French chef must contend with a waitstaff composed of college students, recent immigrants, and participants in the work-release program at the federal correctional facility, and you have all the makings of an unforgettable dining experience.

"Imbecile! If I did not have to wash them afterward, I would choke you with my bare hands!" the chef screamed.

"So, Mother," I asked. "How was your day?"

"I'm not allowed to say," she replied. "I had to sign a confidentiality agreement, remember?"

Seated to my right was Cade. Next to him was Missy Rumpole. Her uncle sat between her and my mother, and Cade's great-grandfather sat next to Mom.

Somehow Gucci the bus driver had managed to join the group, accompanied by a laughing woman named Gypsy. One of the judges also tagged along, a gray-haired man named Bob. He'd brought his cousin, a girl not much older than myself, who introduced herself as Britney.

Three others were crowded around the table, making an unlucky total of thirteen. I'd never met any of them, but one, my mother advised, was Chiquita, the woman responsible for cleaning our room. The other two were first-time tournament fishermen, a middle-aged lawyer named Max Munch and a nice-looking man who asked that we address him simply as Frank.

I later learned that in response to a teenage tipster's phone call, Frank had been sent by the regional FBI office in Kansas City to assist local authorities.

"How nice of you to join us," my mother said politely.

When our waitress, a girl named Rainbow, set thirteen water glasses around the table, Cade spoke up.

"I wouldn't drink that if I were you," he warned.

A Shocking Confession

All eyes at the table turned to Cade.

"There could be a problem with the local water," he said softly, his head down like that of a little kid caught stealing candy.

"Nonsense," declared the lawyer, Max Munch. "That's just an old wives' tale left over from the days when a few ignorant people were fearful of fluoridation."

He chugged the contents of his glass.

"Waitress, another!" he ordered.

"Okey-dokey," Rainbow replied. "It's your funeral."

Narrowing his eyes into a squint, the FBI man, Frank, pushed his water glass away. "I think I'll have a bottled water," he said.

"Not a problem," Rainbow replied. "Anybody else?"

Immediately, eleven other hands went up around the table.

Rainbow pulled out her order pad.

"Twelve cold Ozarkas and one from the swamp," she confirmed. "Got it. Be right back."

"Cade, what's going on?" I demanded to know.

"It's the reservoir," he whispered. "It's got a truck-load of Stink City in it."

"What?" I responded in alarm. "Why would anybody want to do that?"

Once again, he hung his head.

"The plan was to stop the tournament by giving the catfish so much food, they wouldn't bite the hooks," he explained. "At the time, it seemed like a good idea. It never occurred to me that people would be drinking the same water—I swear."

"What the heck did you think a reservoir is for, you lamebrain!" I shouted.

"Shhh!" he said. "Keep your voice down. The walls have ears."

"The walls have grease," I corrected him, "but I don't see how that lets you off the hook."

"Well, don't they clean the water before they put it in the pipes that go to people's houses?" Cade asked naively.

"I'm sure they do the best they can," I said, "but that bait of yours has a lot of secret ingredients. I doubt that the Springfield Water Company is equipped to cope with everything your great-grand-father's dreamed up. Don't forget, he's had one hundred and seven years to experiment."

While I interrogated Cade, Missy Rumpole placed an order for a whole fried catfish with a supersize side of hush puppies, the temperamental chef threw a cabbage at a cowering waiter, a customer started up the jukebox, and a voice cried out from the adjacent bathrooms:

"Gol darn it all, I'm in the wrong one again!"

Meanwhile, Frank remained silent, his elbow on the table, his chin resting in his hand, as if he were enjoying a fascinating show on the radio.

"Why'd you do it, Cade?" I asked, keeping my voice as low as possible.

"I didn't," he whispered. "Not exactly."

"What does that mean?" I pressed him.

"It means I'm the one who gave money to the driver so he'd abandon his truckload of Stink City in front of Miss Hyde's apartment," Cade explained.

"How much did you give him?" I pressed.

"Enough to cover his truck, the shipment, and his first-class airfare to Honduras," Cade confessed, "plus a little extra so he could buy a magazine at the airport."

"Holy smokes!" I exclaimed. "That's a lot of dough."

"I thought I was saving lives," Cade repeated with a sigh.

"Another tap water over here," Max Munch ordered, smacking his empty glass on the table.

Frank grimaced.

"Keep your shirt on, counselor," Rainbow responded. "I've got thirteen mouths at this table and so far yours is not my favorite."

"You do realize, Cade," I pointed out, "you are now a confessed coconspirator in what a lot of people might consider to be an act of environmental terrorism."

Cade slumped down into his seat.

"That's why I need your help," he mumbled.

"Me?" I said. "What can I do?"

"Help me think of something," he answered.

"Cade," I said, "it's pretty obvious that thinking is not something you'll ever be able to do—even with my help."

"There's a lawyer at this table," Cade whispered. "Maybe he could get me off."

"The guy who keeps chugging the lake water?" I replied. "He's an idiot."

Frank sat up, smiled, and nodded his head.

"Let me think," I continued. "To be a criminal, you have to commit a crime. Helping somebody put fishing bait into a fishing lake during a fishing contest may not be nice, but it's not necessarily against the law. I was afraid you were trying to blow up the dam."

"Leigh Ann!" Cade cried. "You know me better than that!"

"Well, I thought I did," I told him, "but after you got mixed up with that witch Miss Hyde, I wasn't so sure anymore."

Cade looked at me with eyes like those of a fresh-caught catfish lying on the dock. As scary as the situation was for the whole dang town, I couldn't help but feel sorry for the kid.

Wising Up

At what age do we stop being stupid?

Sixteen? Twenty-one? Sixty-five? One hundred and seven?

Perhaps I will never know. But in Cade Carlsen's case, it seemed the process had begun.

Interrupting a conversation the old man was having with my mother, I tapped Earl Emerson Carlsen on the arm.

"I know your formula for Stink City is a private matter," I said, "but can you tell me if it consists of all-natural materials?"

"Except for the Old Spice," Cade's great-grandfather replied. "If it weren't for that, I could have the entire concoction certified organic."

"Does this include the nematodes?" I asked.

"I can't confirm the presence of nematodes," he answered. "That's a trade secret."

"Sure thing," I responded. "But they're in there, right?"

"Well," Mr. Carlsen said, thinking it over, "let me put it this way. If a truckload of Stink City catfish bait were to accidentally fall into the Atlantic Ocean, there would be enough nematodes swimming around to clog the Panama Canal."

"Wow!" I exclaimed.

"Yep, but that's just between you and me," he insisted.

"But I can't keep a secret like that!" I told him. "I have to warn people. Human lives could be in danger."

"Now just you hold on a minute, little lady," Earl Emerson Carlsen insisted. "Fish eat those worms like kids eat cheese doodles. Within a day, there's nothing left but a few particles of fish poop. That's the story of a nematode's life. Easy come, easy go."

Frank was paying close attention. Cade breathed a sigh of relief.

"Hey," Cade said suddenly, "I think I forgot to order dinner."

"Honey, let me ask the chef to put something together for you," Rainbow suggested. "He's quite creative."

"Okay, but no catfish. I don't eat catfish," Cade explained.

"Goodness gracious," Rainbow mused. "How did you ever wind up in Springfield?"

"Can't somebody just write the word *MEN* on the door?" a man's voice called from the hall. "How hard would that be?"

"Who chose this place?" Earl Emerson Carlsen inquired.

"The Greater Springfield Invitational Catfish Derby Organizing Committee," my mother replied. "We get to eat here for free."

"Well, if you don't mind my saying so, you get what you pay for," he observed.

"Well, look who walked in the door," I interjected. "The she-devil herself."

Dressed in a bright, flowing flowered muumuu, as if she had been selected to be sacrificed to the gods of the volcano, the capacious Miss Martina Hyde swept into the room and ordered a table for one.

"In your case, lady, may I suggest a table for two?" Rainbow said. "There's no extra charge."

"I'll start with a cocktail," Miss Hyde snapped.

Cade slunk farther down into his chair.

"I don't want her to see me," he explained.

"You know what I'd like to do?" I announced to no one in particular. "I'd like to fish in tomorrow's tournament. Do I need a license or anything?"

Simultaneously, with a flurry of paperwork, the tournament judges at the table produced documents for my signature.

"We'll take care of the rest," they explained.

"How kind of you," I said.

Missy Rumpole, whose uncle had paid for her entry, made a face, which was not that easy to detect, given her nose.

"What do I have to do to get some more water

over here?" Max Munch complained.

"I'm thinking of cutting you off," snapped Rainbow. "But just this once, here, take the whole pitcher."

My mother paid the check using the vouchers we'd received from the Greater Springfield Invitational Catfish Derby Organizing Committee, while others took care of Rainbow's tip. Since there weren't enough vouchers left for another meal, I used the rest at the gift shop to buy a bumper sticker.

FISH FEEL PLAIN, it read. USE TARTAR SAUCE.

Miss Hyde was at her table, dining on barbecued ribs, her eating noises reminiscent of a barnyard animal at a galvanized steel trough. Apparently she never noticed Cade, although later, I learned, she became hopelessly confused by the restrooms.

In the parking lot, Frank stepped over to me.

"Thanks again for dinner," he said.

"All you had was a doughnut," I replied.

"Oh, I got much more than that," he assured me. "And if you don't mind a personal opinion, people who call law enforcement when they suspect a crime are good citizens. And bilking a teenager out of his money is a crime. It's called swindling."

Day of the Serpent

Sing all you wish about April in Paris. Nothing holds a candle to Springfield in May.

The banks of Mud Lake are carpeted with clover—tight white blossoms for the bees, purple ones for the rabbits. In the thickets, fragrant honeysuckle hangs like Spanish moss. Dragonflies, acrobatic masters of the air, dart like fairies over the sparkling water.

If this is what fishing is all about, please disregard what I hypothesized about Jesus and count me in. Surely he would approve of this blissful experience.

Nosey was asleep beside me, his head on a pillow of dandelions, his legs straight up in the air, as he soaked up sunshine on his fuzzy tummy.

I stretched back with my fishing pole between my knees and thought about the present predicament.

I shouldn't have been surprised that Cade had chosen his family's product for his "dramatic public statement." After all, he'd been hinting at such craziness for weeks. But his stunt seemed more a statement to his parents than to the world.

Unless, in some twisted way, he was showing off for Missy Rumpole.

I certainly hoped not.

In my opinion, people shouldn't go to so much trouble to get noticed. All they have to do is stand close enough to smell each other. Pheromones don't lie. Either you are attracted or you are not.

As Max Munch might put it, "Case closed."

My thoughts drifted like the puffy clouds overhead. Gently, I stroked the dozing Nosey's snout.

I read somewhere that dogs can sniff chemical changes in the atmosphere signaling events fifty miles away. Under water, catfish have a similar supersense, with the ability to detect amino acids in dilutions as weak as one part per hundred million. That's like a single grain of sugar dissolved into a hundred thousand backyard pools.

Even from fifteen feet away, under a frozen surface, in the darkness, a catfish can sense a single molecule. Now, a lucky few found themselves in a lake with a truckload of powerful, yummy Stink City catfish bait.

They must be going nuts over those nematodes! I thought.

A butterfly landed on Nosey's tail. The breeze caressed my skin.

Catfish have skin. Unlike other fish, they don't

have protective scales but depend on smooth, slime-covered skin to hold their parts together. This extra sensitivity helps them feel their way through the brush and rocks on lake and river bottoms in the dark.

How sensitive is catfish skin?

One book says, "Flathead catfish seem soothed when they're tickled under the chin or their belly is rubbed."

That's just like Nosey! I thought.

It's obvious: FISH FEEL PAIN®.

And here I was, sitting on the banks of Mud Lake, trying to catch one.

Shame on me! I thought.

Compared to me, the wobbly Cade was as solid as a rock.

Well, I'll just catch one, I told myself. *Then I'll stop.*

A snake, mistaking me for someone fearless, slithered from his hideout underneath a pokeberry bush and made straight for where I was sitting. He was about a five-footer, I'd say, maybe six, but snakes, like fish, enlarge the moment they enter your field of vision.

What I didn't like about this particular snake,

however, was his diamondback pattern and triangular head, telltale signs of a natural born killer. Also, snakes smell with their tongues, and I, for one, didn't care to be snake-sniffed.

I grabbed Nosey and hurried to another spot, high on a limestone boulder, with a clear view of any critters that might be approaching.

Once again I cast my line and lay back down to daydream.

Since the lake's inhabitants had been provided with the ichthyological equivalent of a lifetime supply of Swiss chocolate, I figured eventually they'd be craving something more wholesome. That's why I'd baited my hook with a slice of Granny Smith apple.

Is there such a thing as a lucky snake?

You decide, because all of a sudden something jerked the fishing pole right out of my hands.

Credit for the save goes to Nosey, whose quick, hard-wired reflexes are superior to those of most creatures on this planet. Using his sharp puppy teeth, he snatched the cork handle of the pole as it flew past, then held on tight while I dashed over to relieve him.

Right away, I knew we'd hooked something important: a big hog-nosed turtle, an ancient armored sturgeon, the brother of the Loch Ness monster, or, maybe, just maybe, a prizewinning channel catfish.

Zing went the strings of my monofilament!

Catch As Catch Can

In North America, there are thirty-seven species of catfish, known scientifically as ictalurids. The biggest ictalurids are the blue catfish.

Recently, a fisherman caught a blue catfish in the Mississippi River that weighed one hundred and twenty-four pounds. He tried to donate it to an aquarium, but it died along the way.

Among the smallest catfish are the madtoms.

But for a good time with a hook and line, the most popular catfish are the channel catfish. Channel catfish are America's fish, the most widely distributed sport fish, found everywhere, in every region, in every dark, watery hole.

They are also determined fighters, ferocious biters, crafty adversaries, and a great addition to a cast-iron skillet seasoned with lard.

The largest channel catfish on record is fifty-eight

pounds, but a typical winning fish in a channel cat-fish tournament may weigh in at around twenty pounds.

So anything goes, and may the best person win.

I had fifty feet of line stretched to the limit. Without something to ease the strain, it would surely break. This is why fishermen use flat-bottomed boats, so they can settle back and let the fish tire itself out by dragging the boat around the lake.

Those who fish from the shore are at a decided disadvantage.

Not having experience in such matters, I did what comes naturally. I dived into the water with the pole in my hand.

This did not deter the fish, which had made up its mind to keep going, regardless. Within seconds, I was in over my head, far from the shores of Mud Lake, swallowing Stink City–contaminated lake water.

Despite these setbacks, I didn't let go. A fisherwoman with a fish on the line is a woman possessed.

I suppose I might have drowned, had not I been rescued by the strong arms of a stranger—well, not exactly a stranger, but an unexpected knight of little acquaintance dressed in bright yellow boots.

When he clasped me from behind in a fishlike

Heimlich maneuver, I thought at first it might be Cade Carlsen, but when I turned around I saw the face of Frank, the quiet FBI man from the dinner party.

"Don't let go of the fish, and I won't let go of you," he said. "Together, we'll land this thing, whatever it is."

"You got yourself a deal," I sputtered.

The struggle took us tumbling over hidden rocks and waterlogged logs, but I held on and so did he. Slowly, almost imperceptibly, as the day progressed, the fish wore out. With great respect for its athletic ability and courage, I ultimately brought my finny adversary to shore.

Frank fetched a net, and when we took the fish out of the water, we had to strain to lift together, so heavy was our catch. The FBI agent let out a loud whistle when he saw what we'd landed.

"Well?" I asked. "Is it a catfish? It has whiskers like a catfish, but it's so much uglier than any catfish I've ever seen that I'm thinking it may be something else, like maybe the love child of Miss Martina Hyde."

"Young lady," Frank announced, water sloshing from his boots, "what you have here is the infamous and some say entirely legendary Holy Grail of fresh-water catfish. What you've caught is a rare horned pout."

"A horned pout?" I repeated. "What's a horned pout?"

"A horned pout," Frank explained, in the calm, methodical manner he doubtlessly uses when solving famous cases, "is to the watery world what flying dragons are to the air, what unicorns are to the fields, what fairies are to the woods. The horned pout lives in that realm ruled by magic. The horned pout is nothing less than the King Arthur of catfish."

"Wow!" I said. "Is that lucky?"

"It's very lucky," he confirmed.

"What should I do?" I asked. "Should I make a wish?"

"First thing," Frank instructed, "is to keep it alive. I have a bucket in my truck."

Wouldn't it be easier to keep it alive, I thought, *if we let it go?*

I'm not trained to think like a lawman. When a lawman catches something he's after, he doesn't throw it back.

Frank returned with a steel washtub such as you might use to immerse a large dog in flea dip, followed by a crowd of typical Ozark onlookers. Among these was the Carlsens' handyman, Stretch Glossup, who helped us transfer the fat and furious horned pout into the tub.

Filled with fighting fish and putrid lake water, the container was impossible to move.

"We need a crane," Mr. Glossup suggested.

"Or a front-end loader," a state highway worker piped up. "And I know right where one is. It's government property, but we, the people, are the government, am I right?" he asked, confident that he knew the answer.

The Mud Lake Monster

Word spreads quickly in the Ozarks when the word is horned pout.

(I know, two words.)

Before the highway worker could get back with the hijacked front-end loader, a satellite truck showed up. Painted with the logo of the Channel Catfish Channel, it pulled up beside a row of tour buses and disgorged a guy with perfect hair.

"Holy mackerel!" he gasped into a microphone

while the world got its first glimpse of my rare horned pout. "The Mud Lake Monster is not only real—it's the ugliest thing you ever saw in your life. Whew! And it stinks like an outhouse, too."

After getting similar comments from onlookers, he turned to me, said, "Congratulations," and concluded the live broadcast.

When the front-end loader arrived, Frank asked Mr. Glossup to supervise my fish's bumpy ride to the judge's stand while I fended off financial offers.

"How'd you like to put that thing on display in the Cracker Barrel Restaurant and Gift Shop?" a man in a straw hat asked. "It could be worth a pretty penny."

"I was hoping for more than that," I told him.

"Opportunity knocks," he advised. "When it does, the smart young woman says, 'Who's there?'"

"I'll think about it," I replied.

By now I wanted nothing more than to change out of my wet, muddy, slimy Applecrumble and Fisch clothes and wash my hair.

Back in my hotel room, the only clean clothes I found were khaki shorts. To make an outfit, I charged a T-shirt at the souvenir shop. The slogan read: GET SOME BIG ONES AT MUD LAKE.

Big is a relative term when it comes to catfish. As Miss Hyde revealed when posing as an architect, a big catfish from Thailand may weigh more than six hundred pounds, whereas a big channel catfish from a pond in Pottersville may be only nineteen pounds.

Like *ugly,* or *loud,* or *sweet-smelling, big* is in the senses of the beholder.

Nevertheless, I was plenty curious to find out how much my horned pout weighed. If I couldn't have the catfish crown, I wanted a trophy.

But this is not about me.

I caught up with Cade at the judges' stand, where, thanks to the power of television, the second night's crowd was even bigger than the first. The place was wall to wall with yokels hoping to see a rare horned pout.

Some of them had managed to wangle a spot onstage, including a regional manager of Cracker Barrel, the deputy mayor of Springfield, the owners of a nearby cave, and various other potentates from the Greater Springfield Invitational Catfish Derby Organizing Committee.

"Where's your famous fish?" Cade asked.

"Onstage," I replied. "Unless it's been moved

to make room for more big shots."

"Shouldn't you be up there with them?" he asked.

To my surprise, I heard myself reply, "I think I'd rather be here with you."

Cade looked at me and grinned like a possum.

Although they were eager to be photographed with my fish when it was officially weighed in, none of the dignitaries was willing to touch it, so Mr. Glossup had to heft it out of the tub.

But as I'd found out only a few hours before, that fish was way too much for one person to handle.

With a loud, wet slap, the Mud Lake Monster slipped from Mr. Glossup's hands onto the dangling scale.

Lord, that thing was ugly!

It had a face like a garden gnome's and a fat, bloated body like a prize German sausage. Its tail was tattered, its glassy eyes bulged like an old pug dog's, and it was covered with carbuncular spots, as if it had broken out with acne. With puffy down-turned lips as wide as its head, it greeted the stunned crowd with a permanent scowl.

Officially, my horned pout tipped the scales at sixty-six pounds and six ounces, but I'm sure it weighed more than that before the hot TV lights were turned on. Even from a distance, you could see fish oil baking out of it.

And the odor! Holy smokes! The aroma was prehistoric. You could smell the stink of that smoldering fish from more than a mile away and never again feel like eating.

Heaven help the waitstaff at the Cracker Barrel tonight, I thought.

While the speeches went on and on, with not a single soul mentioning my name, the fish lay listless on the tray of the scale, little x's forming in its eyes. By the time the official from the Springfield fish hatchery got to make his speech, my horned pout wasn't even twitching.

"What we're witnessing is called torture," Cade said. "Come on, Leigh Ann, we've got to save him."

Uh-oh, I thought. *Here we go again!*

Good News Begets the Bad

Cade can't help himself. Maybe that's why he has to help fish.

Pushing and shoving, we made our way to the

deserted stage, where it appeared that my fish was in immediate need of a taxidermist.

"What about that woman who won the Nobel Prize?" Cade asked. "Didn't she have ideas for saving life?"

"You mean Linda Buck?" I answered. "She said nematodes contain something for smell that might also have something to do with how long they live. But she won only half of the Nobel Prize. The other half went to somebody else. So I'm guessing she's only half right."

"Maybe we should feed him nematodes anyway," Cade suggested. "That way, at least he'll have half a chance."

"Okay," I agreed skeptically. "But Linda Buck's field is longevity, not the resurrection of the dead."

"Let's start by putting him in water," Cade said.

We tilted the scale until the horned pout slid like a sticky slab of meat into the tub. Motionless, it floated upside down like a corpse rising from the bottom of a thawing pond.

"This doesn't look very promising," I observed.

"Let's get him to my great-grandfather," Cade said. "He'll know what to do."

It wasn't easy moving my horned pout to the

Fisherman's Inn, but with Cade at the wheel of the front-end loader, we managed. Once inside, we slopped the comatose fish into a bathtub in which only minutes before Nosey had been sleeping.

Cade's great-grandfather came right away.

"Holy sneeze!" the elderly Earl Emerson Carlsen exclaimed. "Does this ever bring back memories!"

"Can anything be done for him?" Cade asked.

"Let me see what I can find at the exhibit," the senior Mr. Carlsen offered. "Meanwhile, boil water."

"For the operation?" I asked.

"For the chowder," he replied.

After a long, worrisome wait, he came back with an armful of Stink City bait.

"Here," he said. "Give him a tablespoon of this every half-hour, and be sure to rub his stomach and scratch behind his ears. They like that."

"Where are his ears?" I asked.

"Just do your best," the old man said.

Cade and I sat up spoon-feeding that godforsaken fish all night long. Throughout the ordeal, the horned pout remained a doornail, but at daybreak it opened one glassy eye, wiggled a fin, and sank to the bottom of the bathtub, where it appeared to be sleeping with the fish.

R.I.P., I thought.

"Keep feeding him," Cade said.

"You feed him," I snapped, exhausted. "I'm going to bed."

It was the third and last day of the Greater Springfield Invitational Catfish Derby, and whatever was going to happen regarding the trophy would happen by four o'clock. I needed my rest.

But peevishness soon produces punishment. That's one of those immutable natural laws, like gravity, or $E=MC^2$, or Horizontal Surfaces Are Soon Piled Up. Turn your back on a friend needing help, and you're justifiably doomed.

The horned pout lived. That's the good news. The Stink City diet agreed with him. In hardly any time at all, he was wowing the Jethros with his ghastly face in the main dining room of the Cracker Barrel Restaurant and Gift Shop on the highway to Branson.

Also, I won the contest. The ceremony was a month late, but tournament officials presented me with a silver trophy nearly three feet tall. In many ways, I felt like Linda Buck, except I didn't have to share my prize.

But that's not what I mean about punishment.

171

You recall Miss Martina Hyde's design for the entrance to the reservoir, her "boat ramp bower," she called it, that judges compared to the St. Louis Arch. And you remember how because of her ignorance of the properties of iron, the sculptures, when cast, weighed two tons each, so instead of dangling in the air like wind chimes they forced their titanium towers to bend all the way to the ground.

As any kid who's ever shot a paper wad at a deserving doofus in math class knows, you can stretch a rubber band only so far before one of two things happens. Either it breaks, snapping against your finger, or it fires with the force of the guns of Navaronne.

Picture the huge sculptures stretching their rods double as if the rods were rubber bands. Then imagine Miss Hyde making one last effort to spoil the derby using her car to shove a stolen cabin cruiser down the linoleum-slick ramp, where she hoped to block the only way in or out until past the judging deadline.

The result, she figured, would be no official winner at all—only Miss Martina Hyde and her FISH FEEL PAIN® bumper stickers.

Now imagine what happens when this woman

can't get her car into gear to prevent sliding down the ramp. Of course, she panics, striking one of the sculptures with her right bumper while slamming its twin with the trailer.

Think back to the rubber band with the paper wad aimed at the nose of Missy Rumpole or whatever other large object you've designated as a target. Consider what happens when someone jostles your hand.

Whap!

Off goes the projectile, to who knows where.

The Flatulent Fog

Brace yourself.

With Miss Hyde's double smacking of her own artwork, the two cast-iron catfish reacted as twin cannonballs. The force of the sliding BMW, the cabin cruiser and trailer, and the pent-up energy contained in the extreme strain on the titanium rods released a pair of two-ton flying fish over the Springfield Catfish Derby grounds like a catapult launching over a poorly defended castle wall. Only in the case of the first fish's destination, the castle had no defense at all. It was made entirely of glass: Stink City's reproduction of the famous Crystal Palace.

That's pretty bad already. But it gets worse.

Remember how the man mixing bait at home blew out his garage door when fumes reached a combustible concentration the moment he lit up a smoke? And remember how the heat intensified inside the Stink City pavilion thanks to its greenhouse-style construction? So here comes a two-thousand-pound cast-iron catfish suddenly thrown from its shackles toward a steaming, gas-filled hothouse. The assault could have been no more complete if conducted by the Royal Fusiliers.

When that first fish hit the Stink City building, it is an understatement to say that it went off like a bomb.

Having failed to contaminate the reservoir, Miss Hyde inadvertently succeeded in sending noxious clouds of catfish bait over three counties, where it plopped to earth onto houses, dairy farms, ponds, hand-dug wells, and roadways like poop from a million flying geese. Shards of glass no bigger than grains of rice rained onto the shores of Mud Lake like winter sleet. The boat ramp was obliterated, of course, as was Miss Hyde's car, and most of the midway.

The second ton of catfish chose a different trajectory. At first it was launched upward, toward the clouds, like the space shuttle, but then, through one of those coincidental quirks of fate that seem so common these days, it returned like a meteorite to obliterate its designer, Miss Martina Hyde.

When finally uncovered, the woman was flatter than a funnel cake.

Ironically, McFunnel's was spared and continued to operate with my mother's voluntary assistance, providing nourishment and hot coffee to emergency workers, the media, and the fishless contestants.

Surprisingly, given the force of the blast, only one other fatality was recorded, and I am sorry to report that it was the locally famous and very wealthy Earl Emerson Carlsen, Cade's curmudgeonly great-grandfather, who'd been locking a document in a fireproof safe when a cast-iron catfish came screaming like a banshee from the skies.

That he lived to be one hundred and seven years old may be consolation for some, but to my way of thinking, loss is loss, at any age.

Perhaps it was, as they say, his time. Or possibly, given his knowledge about the special qualities of nematodes, he could have lived on for many more years. Either way, I was saddened on Cade's behalf and in some ways miss the old man myself.

Cade was never implicated in the trouble, although to my way of thinking, he should have been. But until being stupid becomes a crime, Cade will live his life a free man.

Anyway, truth has little to do with the way things turn out in the world, especially when a handsome FBI man smitten with my mother is writing up the episode's official legal history.

With the death of Miss Hyde, whose identity was confirmed by a loan payment booklet in the BMW's glove compartment, the investigation was closed.

But the fallout was greater than first realized.

A warehouseful of vaporized catfish bait hung around in the atmosphere, dripping goo and spreading Carlsenstink throughout the city.

"The flatulent fog," the *Pottersville Post* declared.

With migrating waterfowl felled by the smell, snakes turned as straight as yardsticks, and the only ivory-billed woodpecker in generations keeled over and petrified like a yule log, Greater Springfield was declared an environmental disaster area.

Have you noticed how people like to say, "The solution came from an unlikely source," as if only Benjamin Franklin, Thomas Edison, or Stephen Hawking could have figured out how to solve a problem? In the case of the Springfield Stink Bomb, the solution came from a very likely source, albeit previously unknown to the community: the Carlsens' handyman's domestic housekeeper, an elderly, gold-toothed woman named Etta, whose last name Mr. Glossup had never bothered to find out.

Etta's idea was at once brilliant, proven, and comprehensive. There was no need to wait for a government feasibility study. Everybody knew it would work.

"Lemon juice," Etta said. "You use it on fish to make fish smell less fishy. Works good with shrimps, too."

"I find lemon juice somewhat tart," the mayor's wife objected. "Why not something sweeter, more fragrant, like flowers?"

"You'll get plenty of flowers at your funeral, girlfriend," Etta pointed out. "In the meantime, somebody's got to clean up this stinking town."

Miracle Juice

Lemon.

After years of digression into orange, berry, honeysuckle, lilac, and green apple, it's still America's favorite smell for consumer cleaning products.

Lemon's citric acid is also one of those basic molecules, like vinegar—a building block of life.

But lemons aren't free, and neither is the cost of shipping them to Springfield from the climes where they originate, or the cost of labor to slice them in half, cover with dainty circles of cheesecloth, and squeeze in liberal doses throughout the city.

Sensing a once-in-a-lifetime opportunity, Etta rounded up a posse of relatives, ex-husbands, and recently released friends who were willing to work for twice the minimum wage plus benefits and beer. The surviving adult Carlsens, Lenny and Lani, although publicly bereft over the loss of the family patriarch, volunteered to contribute funds for the cleanup in exchange for the permits and tax breaks needed to move their manufacturing plant from their home to an abandoned Titan missile silo complex west of Pottersville.

Watching them work the system was like

observing plate spinners at the circus, skillful jugglers spinning deals within deals while telling jokes, making wisecracks, and changing the subject.

Etta was even better than her betters. Before the deal was done, she'd convinced Mr. Glossup to buy her a brand-new BMW, one just like the late Miss Martina Hyde's.

Other than to express my regrets, I've been avoiding saying anything about the death of Earl Emerson Carlsen. It's a tough subject for me to address, for a couple of reasons.

First of all, I care about Cade. He and his great-grandfather were quite close.

Then there's the other thing.

The document that he placed into the fireproof safe the night the Stink City pavilion was attacked by a hurling cast-iron catfish was a last will and testament, as if the old man knew his time was up.

The will had been drawn up by the lawyer Max Munch, witnessed by the lady from McFunnel's, and notarized by Pottersville letter carrier Debra Dogwald, who'd driven all the way to Springfield to deliver what turned out to be Earl Emerson Carlsen's final order of laboratory-quality nematodes.

Under the circumstances, no one doubted that, while slightly degraded around the edges like the Declaration of Independence, the senior Mr. Carlsen's will was a valid document.

But let's get something straight. I've told you over and over that this is not about me, it's about Cade. It's also not about Cade's great-grandfather.

If I had written on page one that the story you are about to read is about a 107-year-old man who smells like a dead skunk, tell me, would you have bothered to read any further?

Of course not.

Old is old and dead is dead and long gone is long gone. So I, for one, will stiffen my spine and shed no more tears over Earl Emerson Carlsen. He had his successes, he had his quirks, and in the final moments of his extraordinarily long life, he apparently had a soft spot for me.

He left me something really special. (Okay, two things.)

His vast fortune, his bank accounts, his stocks and bonds, his land, and his company went to Lenny and Lani, as was only right.

His cattle futures went to Cade, for college expenses.

But these gifts pale when compared to what he bequeathed to me. First, he left me the crown from the first Springfield Catfish Derby ever held, when he was named King Catfish. He'd kept it in a safe-deposit box all these years.

It's fourteen-karet gold, with real diamonds, emeralds, and rubies swirled in a pattern like a comet.

I love it.

The other thing he bequeathed to me was sealed with embossed red wax in a large glassine envelope: the only copy of the formula for Stink City brand catfish bait, a secret that includes a processed essence of nematodes, a life-extending ingredient that Linda Buck suspects but as of yet has failed to discover.

There was also a handwritten note.

"Dear Leigh Ann," it said. "For the good of mankind, wait many, many years to reveal the enclosed information. Especially the part about the nematodes. I've lived longer than I had a right to, and have progeny who should have been thrown over the White River Bridge in burlap bags at birth.

"You, however, will know when the time is right to share my accidental discovery. Until then, wear your crown, your smile, and your kind disposition, and whenever you get the chance, please watch after my beloved but misguided great-grandson.

"Sincerely, Earl Emerson Carlsen."

Longevity is not the same as immortality.

A cast-iron two-thousand-pound replica of a Bangkok catfish crashing into a methane bomb is enough to change your fortune for all time.

I kept my word.

I didn't tell a single soul. Not Cade. Not my mother. Not even Nosey.

Life Goes On

That's about it.

Cade's parents went nuts with their newfound wealth. They built a big factory far from town—and far from our home, thank goodness—hired people from distant lands, and produced a concoction called Stink City Catfish Bait that was missing its principal secret ingredient. Apparently, it didn't matter. The product smelled as bad as ever, and its reputation was sufficient to assure the brand's success for many years.

Believing is as good as being true.

And Cade no longer needed to work there.

As a result, he began to smell like a regular kid.

In fact, after I bought him a spritzer of cologne, he smelled pretty good.

His personal bus driver, Gucci, was reassigned to be foreman at the new plant, which pleased the perpetually confused Gucci but annoyed the loyal servant Mr. Glossup, who figured the job should have been his.

Instead, the Carlsens let him go. Within the week, Mr. Glossup had taken a job at the prestigious architectural firm of Van Cleef & Arpels, guarding the office supplies.

There were a few problems with Etta's cure. The lemon juice upset the stomachs of nearly all the armadillos, none of which were native to the region. They threw up on the highways and backroads, creating a stink slick that, like an ice storm, caused numerous automobile accidents.

Who knew?

A handful of other animals were also affected.

Goldfinches tumbled from trees like autumn leaves.

Toads bloated up and exploded.

The fire department hosed spiders, mosquitoes, and horseflies into the gutters like so many bits of cottonwood fluff.

The runaway dogs simply left. With no high-quality stink to attract them to Pottersville, they packed up their mangy packs and moved on to Houston, where, I'm told, the olfactory pickings remain excellent to this very day.

Perhaps most surprisingly, the Springfield Catfish Derby became a bigger event than ever, besting the competing derbies in Louisiana, Mississippi, and Tennessee.

The reason was this: Following the widespread application of lemon juice, anglers were awarded cash prizes for catching catfish that, instead of weighing the most, tasted the best.

With such a heavy dose of lemon juice, every Springfield-area catfish was well prepared for cooking.

The Channel Catfish Channel signed a partnership agreement with the Food Network to cover the event. It was tailor-made for TV. Not a moment went by that there wasn't some new delicious surprise.

Lenny and Lani's most successful brand extension

was the Stink City automatic catfish cornmeal-breading machine.

"You just stick the catfish in one end and it comes out ready for the skillet in the other," they explained.

The lawyer Max Munch, the one who at the Crazy Cajun Catfish Cafe drank tap water like it was his last day on earth, kept getting younger. Recently, on television, he appeared to be twenty-five years old. He claimed it was due to daily exercise and decent living. Of course, it was the essence of nematodes in the Springfield water.

Frank came to town and took my mother to the new romantic catfish restaurant on the square in downtown Pottersville—Barbels, Books & Candles. They were gone for more than four hours.

I got a nice long letter from the Nobel laureate Linda Buck. In it she asked if there was anything peculiar going on in the region that she might want to know about. I replied that Missy Rumpole had finally gotten her nosefixed, and that my dog's life, measured in the seven-year increments called dog years, was now a minus three, thanks to a diet of Mighty Dog and fresh-squeezed nematodes.

Few people in the area seemed to be getting older. Surprisingly, Linda Buck never wrote back. I guess she was preoccupied with her worm research. Or maybe it was the continuing embarrassment of having to share a prize with a man. I can only imagine what that must feel like.

(Once, early on, the thought crossed my mind to share my prize with Frank, but I quickly dismissed it.)

But there are some things about people you shouldn't try to change. Some people like to eat catfish. Some don't. Some people are smart. Some are less so. That's just the way it is. If you want to get along with somebody, you have to let him be.

When Cade turned sixteen, despite his baby face he got his driver's license and a car, a sensible hybrid convertible. On nice days, of which we have plenty in Pottersville, we like to put the top down and smell the wonderful Ozark summer.

Dusty roads. Blackberries. Grasshoppers. Horses and cows.

I like Cade. Honestly, I do.

He's no genius, but he's sensitive and trainable. He drives within the speed limit. He wears his seat belt. He signals for every turn.

His new car has a bumper sticker on the back.

It says: HAVE YOU HUGGED YOUR FISH TODAY?®